THEOPHILUS NORTH

by
Matthew Burnett

Based on the novel by
Thornton Wilder

SAMUEL FRENCH, INC.

45 West 25th Street
NEW YORK 10010
LONDON

7623 Sunset Boulevard
HOLLYWOOD 90046
TORONTO

BILLING AND CREDIT REQUIREMENTS

All producers of *THEOPHILUS NORTH must* give credit to the Author of the Play and the Author of the Novel in all programs distributed in connection with performances of the Play and in all instances in which the title of the Play appears for purposes of advertising, publicizing or otherwise exploiting the Play and/or a production. The name of the Author of the Play *must* appear on a separate line on which no other name appears, immediately following the title, and *must* appear in size of type not less than fifty percent the size of the title type. The name of the Author of the Novel must appear on a separate line immediately below the name of the Author of the Play in a size of type equal to that of the Author of the Play, wherever and whenever the Author of the Play receives credit.

In addition, the following credit must appear in all programs distributed in connection with the Work:

THEOPHILUS NORTH
Originally produced on January 24, 2003 by
Geva Theatre Center, Rochester, NY
Mark Cuddy, Artistic Director
and
Arena Stage, Washington, D.C.
Molly D. Smith, Artistic Director
Stephen Richard, Executive Director

PRODUCTION HISTORY

THEOPHILUS NORTH was originally produced by Geva Theatre Center, Rochester, NY, Mark Cuddy, Artistic Director, and Arena Stage, Washington D.C., Molly D. Smith, Artistic Director, Stephen Richard, Executive Director, with an opening night performance on January 24, 2003. It was directed by Mark Cuddy, with choreography by Terry Berliner, set and costume design by G.W. Mercier, lighting design by Ann G. Wrightson, original music by Gregg Coffin, dramaturgy by Marge Betley, stage management by Kathleen Horton Mahan, assistant stage management by Joseph Knight, and technical direction by Jim Glendinning. The cast consisted of Matthew Floyd Miller as Theophilus, with Valerie Leonard (Woman 2), Siobhan Mahoney (Woman 1), Lynn Steinmetz (Woman 3), Edward James Hyland (Man 3), Michael Laurino (Man 1), and Andrew Polk (Man 2).

The New York City premiere of *THEOPHILUS NORTH* was produced by Keen Company, Carl Forsman, Artistic Director, Wayne Kelton, Producer, at the Clurman Theatre, Theatre Row, with an opening night performance on September 14, 2006. It was directed by Carl Forsman, with scenic design by Beowulf Borritt, costume design by Theresa Squire, lighting design by Josh Bradford, sound design by Daniel Baker, stage management by Erin Grenier. The cast *(in order of appearance)* was as follows: Virginia Kull (Woman 1), Giorgio Litt (Theophilus North), Geddeth Smith (Man 3), Margaret Daly (Woman 3), Joe Delafield (Man 1), Regan Thomspson (Woman 2), and Brian Hutchison (Man 2).

CHARACTERS

Theophilus North
Man 1
Woman 1
Man 2
Woman 2
Man 3
Woman 3

The "men" and "women" in the play will portray all characters that come in contact with Theophilus in this story. The actor playing Theophilus should play *only* Theophilus. The breakdown of roles for the six Men and Women is as follows:

Man 1 *(Late 20s)*
Man 1
Bill Wentworth
Charles Fenwick
George Granberry

Woman 1 *(Mid 20s)*
Woman 1
Eloise Fenwick
Diana Bell

Man 2 *(Mid 30s)*
Man 2
Henry Simmons
Hilary Jones
Willis

Woman 2 *(Mid 30s)*
Woman 2
Mrs. Fenwick
Myra Granberry
Mrs. Sarah Bosworth

Man 3 *(60s)*
Man 3
Father
Josiah Dexter
Augustus Bell
Dr. James Bosworth

Woman 3 *(50s)*
Woman 3
Mother
Mrs. Cranston
Cora Cummings

AUTHOR'S NOTE

The set should be simple, offering an easy, uncomplicated playing area, in order to move the action from one location to another
rapidly.

Props should be minimal or mimed. Furniture should be minimal
and not necessarily realistic. However, a real period stationary
bicycle for Theophilus and actual books should be utilized. Costumes, as well, should be as simple as possible. A basic costume
suggesting the time and place of the piece are necessary for each
of the "Men" and "Women." But as there are multiple roles for
each of these actors and quick changes will be necessary, I suggest simple accessories (or even *one* accessory) which will read-
ily identify the character. The ability for fast alterations to the
basic costume is also desirable. As representatives of the various
areas of Newport, it may be assumed that the Men and Women
speak "Out."

Translations of the scenes conducted in French can be found following the text of the play.

THEOPHILUS NORTH was written to be performed by seven
professional actors. However, recognizing that some community,
amateur, or other nonprofessional groups with larger casting
needs may desire to have characters played by individual actors, I
approve of it entirely. At that point the division of roles, as well
as the lines for "Men," "Women," and places, is at the discretion
of the director.

ACT I

Scene 1
The Nine Ambitions

(WOMAN 1 appears.)

WOMAN 1. It was the spring of 1926. Slowly and wonderingly one raises one's head.

(She goes.)

THEOPHILUS. *(Entering)* I quit! I quit, I quit, I quit! I, Theophilus North, quit my job! *(Out)* Haven't you ever wanted to? I feel like I've been released from a hospital after a protracted illness. For thirty years I've been plagued by a life of auxiliary verbs: "should" and "ought." The time has come for me to dive into the world and rejoice at the ripples I make. My mind is alive with options, as well as with the voices of my parents and their inevitable reactions.

(MOTHER and FATHER appear.)

MOTHER. You did what?
FATHER. Have you been drinking?
MOTHER. How could you do that?
THEOPHILUS. Easily. I walked into the main office and

said, "I quit."

FATHER. Watch your tone.

THEOPHILUS. *(Out)* My father. His overstanding underwhelms me.

MOTHER. But you love teaching.

THEOPHILUS. Teaching is a safety net for indeterminate natures.

MOTHER. But you have such a gift for it.

THEOPHILUS. *(Out)* My mother will now recite an "Ode to Complacency."

MOTHER. Maybe if you asked nicely they'd give you your job back.

THEOPHILUS. I'm almost *thirty*. I have been teaching and tutoring at this damn—

FATHER. Language—

THEOPHILUS. —prep school and summer camp in New Jersey for four years.

FATHER. Four and a half.

THEOPHILUS. *(Deferential sarcasm)* Thank you. I don't know what I want to do, but I don't want to be *there* anymore.

MOTHER. But you love those boys.

THEOPHILUS. You try sleeping in a tent with ten urchins—

FATHER. Tone—

THEOPHILUS. —during the phase when everything forbidden obsesses them. Giggling for half an hour every time one of them—

FATHER. Language—

THEOPHILUS. —well, every time some little physiological accident occurs.

FATHER. Quitters never prosper.

THEOPHILUS. No, Poppa, *cheaters* never prosper. Quitters

never *win.*

FATHER. So that makes you...

THEOPHILUS. Unencumbered.

FATHER. *(To MOTHER)* He *has* been drinking.

MOTHER. What will you do?

THEOPHILUS. I don't know. Something. I don't know! I have ambition. *(Out)* As a matter of fact—

FATHER. Oh, God...

MOTHER. Language...

THEOPHILUS. *(Out)* At various times I've been afire with nine Life Ambitions. I'll tell you about them.

FATHER. Must you?

THEOPHILUS. Yes. In random order they have been: Anthropologist, Archeologist, Saint, Detective, Magician, Actor—

FATHER. Sweet mercy...

THEOPHILUS. Lover, Rascal. Which all lead to my last and overriding ambition: to be a Free Man.

FATHER. What's wrong with being a banker?

MOTHER. Or a lawyer?

THEOPHILUS. I don't want any career bound up with directorates and boards of governors. I want no boss over me. After four-and-a-half years of confinement I want adventure, risk, fun, danger. I want to comb the earth, read a million faces, intervene in life.

FATHER. And how do you intend on accomplishing this "circumnavigation of fun?"

THEOPHILUS. I've bought a used car from Eddie Linley for twenty-five dollars. Her name...

HANNAH (WOMAN 2). *(Appearing)* Hannah. From the song. *(Sings)* "Hard-Hearted Hannah!"

THEOPHILUS. Feeling up to a trip, Hannah?

HANNAH. I long to lie down in a New Jersey gully, but Eddie keeps resuscitating me.

THEOPHILUS. And now you are my chariot to real life!

HANNAH. All right. Where to?

THEOPHILUS. Well, I have been to Paris, but I long to visit so many other major cities: Rome and Budapest, Hong Kong and Shanghai, London, Berlin...

HANNAH. New York is close. How about New York?

THEOPHILUS. New York! The most wonderful city in the world. Persons living there are animated by a galvanic force.

HANNAH. I think I could manage New York.

THEOPHILUS. Yes, but Hannah, convenience rarely leads to adventure. I've already *been* to New York. I've got my own car, no obligations, and the roads of the entire planet before me.

HANNAH. So?

THEOPHILUS. I'll be true to my name... and go north!

Scene 2
Newport

(THEOPHILUS sees a sign.)

MAN 1. "Newport, 30 Miles."

(He goes.)

HANNAH. Newport?

THEOPHILUS. Why not? Yes. I'll swing through Newport, where my brother served ten years ago in the Coast Artillery. So it's off to Newport on the island of Aquidneck. Ah, sweet freedom!

(Sees another sign.)

WOMAN 3. "Welcome to Newport."

(She goes. HANNAH begins to cough violently.)

THEOPHILUS. Come on, Hannah.
HANNAH. Nope, I'm done. Stop me over there.

(JOSIAH appears.)

JOSIAH. "Josiah Dexter's Garage. Repairs."
THEOPHILUS. Will you examine her while I use a telephone?
MAN 2. *(Appearing)* Young Men's Christian Association.
THEOPHILUS. I am inquiring if there is a room available. My name is Theophilus North. I am thirty, was christened in the First Congregational Church of Madison, Wisconsin, I am fairly sociable—
MAN 2. That's all right buddy, calm down. Fifty cents a night.

(He goes.)

THEOPHILUS. *(To JOSIAH.)* How much?
JOSIAH. Fifteen dollars looks like.

THEOPHILUS. Do you buy old cars?

JOSIAH. Yes.

THEOPHILUS. I'll sell it to you for twenty if you'll drive my luggage to the "Y."

JOSIAH. Agreed.

THEOPHILUS. Good-bye, Hannah. No hard feelings on either side.

HANNAH. Happens to the best of us, dear.

THEOPHILUS. "Balde ruhest du auch."

(HANNAH goes.)

JOSIAH. Had the car long?

THEOPHILUS. Seven hours and thirty-five minutes.

JOSIAH. May I ask what it was you said to the car?

THEOPHILUS. Goethe. "Balde ruhest du auch." "Soon you too will rest."

JOSIAH. Do you get that worked up about everything you own?

THEOPHILUS. Mr. Dexter, I have been in Newport for a quarter of an hour. I'm happy to be anywhere other than where I was. I'm a little light-headed.

JOSIAH. Where you from?

THEOPHILUS. New Jersey.

JOSIAH. Where you headed?

THEOPHILUS. Off to see the world.

JOSIAH. Well, congratulations. You've seen 180 miles of it.

THEOPHILUS. Who rents bicycles around here?

JOSIAH. I do.

THEOPHILUS. Would you pick one for me?

JOSIAH. All right.

THEOPHILUS. Has my light-headedness offended you, Mr. Dexter?

JOSIAH. We New Englanders don't go in for light-headedness much, but I've heard nothing to be offended at. There's your bicycle. *(A bicycle appears. It is stationary.)* Good day to you.

(He goes.)

THEOPHILUS. *(Hopping onto the bicycle and peddling. Out)* Down Main Street and out!

(MEN 1 and 2, WOMEN 1, 2 and 3 appear and go, in turn.)

MAN 1. Over here, Theophilus! Ride on the Avenue, peddle down Thames Street!

WOMAN 2. To me: the Ten-Mile Drive along the bay. Each mile more sublime than the last.

MAN 2. Here, Theophilus! Ride beneath these!

WOMAN 3. *(As they open green umbrellas.)* The trees of Newport.

MAN 2. Brought from exotic locations around the world by scientists and yachtsman.

THEOPHILUS. Remarkable!

WOMAN 1. To me, Theophilus. The Brenton Point Lighthouse. Climb the steps to the viewing deck. Feel the wind in your face as you gaze across the glittering sea. On a clear day, what can be seen will amaze you!

THEOPHILUS. Yes, I see! What is it?

WOMAN 1. Portugal.

THEOPHILUS. What a remarkable thing is a lighthouse!

Raised high above the world to see the arc of the horizon and recognize limitless options! Now there's an example to hold close at hand.

WOMAN 1. Indeed. Where are you going?

THEOPHILUS. To call on an old friend of the family.

(She goes as scene shifts to Bill Wentworth's office.)

BILL. *(Out)* Bill Wentworth, Superintendent of the Newport Casino and Tennis Club. A friend of his brother's who once won a tennis tournament here. *(To THEOPHILUS)* Theophilus, great to see you. What brings you to our fair island?

THEOPHILUS. Off to conquer the world, Mr. Wentworth.

BILL. Bill.

THEOPHILUS. Bill. But I'm waylaid here for a week or two, so I'm going to try and earn some money. I find myself like Columbus, seeking funds in Ferdinand's court before the great voyage.

BILL. Hey, why don't you sit here and type up an advertisement of your skills. We can call it in to the newspaper and I'll tack a copy of it on the Casino's bulletin board.

THEOPHILUS. Oh. Thanks.

BILL. Sure. We always have young people during the summer who need tutoring. We have another group that might be eager for your services, too. Would you be ready to read aloud to older people with poor eyesight?

THEOPHILUS. Certainly.

BILL. And could you coach tennis to children between eight and fifteen?

THEOPHILUS. I suppose.

BILL. Good. I'll start collecting a class for you. A dime an hour for each youngster. If you didn't bring any tennis gear with you, there's a room back there filled with racquets, flannels and shoes. Type up your ad. I've got to go and see what my carpenters are doing. *(Out)* Kindness is not entirely uncommon.

(BILL exits.)

THEOPHILUS. *(Out)* But imaginative kindness can give a man a shock. Within four days I have pupils on the courts and I sound like I know what I'm doing, thanks to some old copies of

MAN 2. "Tennis for Beginners"

THEOPHILUS. which I found at the Casino. Within a week telephone calls arrive, my advertisement having exposed me to "the lunatic fringe" of the general public.

LUNATIC (MAN 3). We know you are a German spy and we have our eyes on you.

2nd LUNATIC (WOMAN 1). Mr. North? This is Mrs. Denby's secretary speaking.

THEOPHILUS. *(Out)* For some reason, I am more outspoken and even rude over the telephone than in person.

2nd LUNATIC. Mrs. Denby wishes to know if you would be able to read aloud to her three children between the hours of 3:30 and 6:30 on Thursday afternoons?

THEOPHILUS. Thank Mrs. Denby and tell her that it is impossible to hold *one* child's attention on a book for longer than forty minutes. I suggest they be encouraged to play with matches.

LUNATIC. Oh!

SARAH BOSWORTH. Mr. North? *(With great arrogance)* This is Mrs. Sarah McHenry Bosworth. *(Pause. Out)* I pause to let him savor the richness of his privilege.

THEOPHILUS. Yes, ma'am.

SARAH. My father would like to discuss with you the possibility of your reading to him. Philosophy and the *Bible*. The entire *Bible*. He has read it eleven times and wishes to know if you are able to read rapidly. He would like to break his record of forty-eight hours.

THEOPHILUS. Tempting as it is, Mrs. Bosworth, I fear that a vocal sprint through the "Book of Joshua" is an invitation to injury, and I must decline. Goodbye. *(He hangs up on her. Out)* My days are soon filled with tennis lessons and readings. I find myself cycling up and down the Avenue like a delivery boy beneath the shade of Newport's greenery.

(MAN 3 appears.)

MAN 3. Across the street from the Tennis Casino you will find me: a small public park. I comprise nine beech trees, three poplar, and an odd stone structure. Most mistake it for some abandoned project, but look closely. It is a stone round tower, built by the Vikings—or by Benedict Arnold's grandfather. There's still some disagreement. Either way, it is one of the few remaining vestiges from the 17th century village of Newport's first settlers.

Cities and persons are like trees: the sap first rising in the early years becomes its future contour. Small traces allude to the mystery of what things were, are, and what they may become.

(He goes.)

THEOPHILUS. "The mystery of what we may become..."

Scene 3
The Fenwicks, i

THEOPHILUS. *(Out)* But there is no mystery about who my favorite pupil is in the early morning tennis class: Eloise Fenwick.

(ELOISE is revealed.)

THEOPHILUS. She is fourteen. Which means, of course, she can be any age between ten and sixty, as the spirit moves her. Some days on the court I have to drag her to the back line. Other days she precedes me, Countess of Aquidneck and the Adjacent Isles. She is intelligent, deep and able to keep her counsel; beautiful and shows no signs of knowing it. It's like having a friendship with one of Shakespeare's heroines at the age of fourteen.

ELOISE. I wish my brother Charles would take lessons with you.

THEOPHILUS. But Charles is sixteen. Mr. Dobbs teaches that age group.

ELOISE. He doesn't like Mr. Dobbs. He doesn't like anybody. He just practices against the wall over there by himself. No ----I wish you would teach him something.

THEOPHILUS. Well, I can't until I'm asked, can I?

ELOISE. I know. Mama wants you to help Charles with his French. She's going to ask you today after the lesson. She's over there, in the gallery. The one wearing all the veils.

(MRS. FENWICK is revealed.)

THEOPHILUS. *(With suspicion)* Eloise.

ELOISE. She's motoring today. Come on, I'll introduce you. I just hope you're better at French than you are at tennis. Mama, this is Mr. North. The gentleman I was telling you about. Mr. North, this my mother.

THEOPHILUS. Very pleased to make your acquaintance, Mrs. Fenwick.

MRS. FENWICK. My pleasure, Mr. North. Eloise, go tell your brother to wait after he's through. *(ELOISE exits.)* Mr. North, you have an interesting approach to teaching tennis.

THEOPHILUS. Do you think so?

MRS. FENWICK. I do. At what point will you begin demonstrating to Eloise how to get the ball *over* the net?

THEOPHILUS. Don't worry. The regular coach returns in June.

MRS. FENWICK. *(Smiling)* It doesn't really concern me, Mr. North. Your name is often mentioned in my house. Eloise admires you very much.

THEOPHILUS. I had dared not hope so.

MRS. FENWICK. I wanted to talk to you about my son Charles. I was hoping that you could find time to coach him in French. He speaks the language, but has a "bloc" against genders and tenses. He admires everything French.

THEOPHILUS. Mrs. Fenwick, I have taught French to many students. It is like dragging stones uphill. I would like to have a short talk with Charles and hear his own expression of interest.

MRS. FENWICK. That is a good deal to ask of Charles Fenwick... I find it difficult to tell you this—to describe certain... traits... in Charles. But I feel I must.... He has a disdain, almost a contempt for everyone he has come in contact with, except perhaps Eloise and a few priests. I have found the courage to give it a name. *(Pause)* He is a snob. An unbounded snob.

THEOPHILUS. I see.

MRS. FENWICK. He has never said "Thank you" to a servant, not once, and the few times he has thanked his father or myself have been barely audible. He takes no interest in any subject but one—our social standing. Is his father in the best clubs? Are we invited to important occasions? He is driving us mad.

THEOPHILUS. Can Eloise persuade him to talk to me now for a few minutes?

MRS. FENWICK. Eloise can persuade him to do anything.

(She exits. CHARLES appears.)

THEOPHILUS. *(To CHARLES)* Mr. Fenwick—I shall call you that at the beginning of our conversation, then I shall call you Charles—Eloise tells me that you have had several years of French? *(Silence)* Well, probably all you need is a few weeks polishing the irregular verbs. *(Silence)* I have been told a number of things about you, do you have any questions about me?

(Pause)

CHARLES. Is it true that you went to Yale?
THEOPHILUS. Yes.

(Pause)

CHARLES. If you went to Yale, why are you working here?
THEOPHILUS. To make some money.
CHARLES. You don't look... poor.
THEOPHILUS. Oh, yes, I'm very poor, Charles.
CHARLES. I know why. You're the worst tennis instructor

I've ever seen.

THEOPHILUS. I may be poor, Charles, but I'm cheerful.

CHARLES. Did you belong to any of those fraternities or clubs at Yale?

THEOPHILUS. A few, but I was not a member of any of the Senior Societies.

CHARLES. *(Looking at THEOPHILUS)* Did you try to get into one?

THEOPHILUS. Trying has nothing to do with it. They did not invite me. What kind of clubs would you like to be a member of, Charles? *(Silence)* You know, there's a famous club in Baltimore, that must be the most delightful in the world and the hardest to get into.

CHARLES. What is it?

THEOPHILUS. It's called the "Catgut Club." Around Johns Hopkins Medical School there are great doctors and eminent professors who belong to the "Catgut," because they're also accomplished musicians. Every Tuesday night they play chamber music.

CHARLES. What?

THEOPHILUS. Chamber music. Do you know what that is? *(CHARLES reacts.)* Charles, are you unwell? Your neck has turned red. I said chamber music, not chamber pots! *(CHARLES reacts.)* Charles, there's another club, also very select, at Saratoga Springs, whose members own racehorses, but very seldom ride them. They call it the "Horses and Asses Club"—the members don't sit on their horses, they sit on their asses. *(CHARLES reacts.)* Which club would you rather belong to?

CHARLES. The... I, uh... Uh—

THEOPHILUS. Never mind, I'm wasting your time. Are you ready to say that you'll work with me on the finer points of

French? Be frank with me, Charles.

CHARLES. *(Swallowing)* Yes, sir.

THEOPHILUS. Fine. I'll wait until your mother returns. I don't want to interrupt your practice any longer. *(He puts out his hand; CHARLES shakes it.)* Don't tell that little story about Saratoga Springs where it might cause any embarrassment. It's all right, just among men.

(CHARLES exits as MRS. FENWICK enters.)

THEOPHILUS. Charles feels that he'd like to try a little coaching.

MRS. FENWICK. Oh, I'm so relieved!

THEOPHILUS. Mrs. Fenwick, my next lesson begins shortly. May I be brief?

MRS. FENWICK. Please.

THEOPHILUS. And somewhat blunt?

MRS. FENWICK. I have been married nearly eighteen years and have two children, Mr. North. I don't shock the way I used to.

THEOPHILUS. I was speaking to Charles about music, and said the word "chamber."

MRS. FENWICK. Yes?

THEOPHILUS. Having worked with young boys I believe that every slightly suggestive word is invested with the horror and excitement of the forbidden.

MRS. FENWICK. What has this to do with my son? He's sixteen.

THEOPHILUS. Precisely. Does Charles have any association with boys his own age?

MRS. FENWICK. Practically none.

THEOPHILUS. Does he giggle?

MRS. FENWICK. Charles?!

THEOPHILUS. Whisper?

MRS. FENWICK. Hardly.

THEOPHILUS. Shout?

MRS. FENWICK. Never.

THEOPHILUS. Horseplay?

MRS. FENWICK. None.

THEOPHILUS. Mrs. Fenwick, Charles is trapped in a phase of development he should have outgrown by twelve.

MRS. FENWICK. I see. And what I called his "snobbery"...

THEOPHILUS. Is an escape into a world without embarrassment.

MRS. FENWICK. My dear Charles.

THEOPHILUS. Don't be too upset, Mrs. Fenwick. I can assure you that Mozart had the same problem.

MRS. FENWICK. Charles and Mozart!? Do you believe that Mozart outgrew his childishness?

THEOPHILUS. No.

MRS. FENWICK. Oh, Mr. North, I've hated every word you've said, yet I can see that you're probably right. But do you know what to do?

THEOPHILUS. Absolutely. I know exactly what to do. *(Out)* I have no idea what to do. But when in doubt, act twice as certain.

MRS. FENWICK. How can you be so sure, Mr. North? You are not a doctor.

THEOPHILUS. No, Mrs. Fenwick, I am not. But I don't think Charles needs a doctor. What he needs is a slightly older friend to help guide him through some murky territory. That is a role I am willing to play. May I go forward with my plan, even if it is unorthodox?

MRS. FENWICK. I must discuss it with Mr. Fenwick and Father Walsh. Mr. North, this has been a painful conversation for me. You will hear from me. Good morning.

(She exits.)

Scene 4
Herman's

THEOPHILUS. *(Out)* Having breathed the rarified air of Charles Fenwick's presence, I need some grounding among my fellow "commoners." And this is where I land:

HERMAN (MAN 3). *(Out)* Herman's Billiard Parlor. Seven tables and a bar dispensing licit beverages, but any strong drink you bring in your own pocket is winked at. Most of the customers here are servants of one kind or another. *(Indicating THEOPHI-LUS)* Except that one. None of us is sure about that one.

(He goes, as HENRY SIMMONS—a Cockney—appears.)

HENRY. You there, professor!
THEOPHILUS. What?
HENRY. You kind of stand out. Feeling ostrich-sized?
THEOPHILUS. There is a tangible coolness.
HENRY. How about a drink with me? What's your name, cully? Ted North?

THEOPHILUS. Theophilus. How did you know that?

HENRY. *(Taking a flask from his pocket)* New face, saw your ad... and servants like to talk, Ted. Mine's Henry Simmons.

THEOPHILUS. How do you do, Henry?

HENRY. Alright, I guess. A little idle, which drives a man crazy. You see, I'm a "gentleman's gentleman" and Mr. Forrester is in Tierra del Fuego taking pictures of birds. And my ladyfriend, Edweena, is a lady's maid on a yacht right now going through the Bahamas. Now who are you, Ted, and are you happy and well?

THEOPHILUS. *(Out)* I don't know why, but I tell him the story of my life, ending up with my being temporarily stranded in Newport.

HENRY. Teddie, there's a lot of suspicion, distrust, of newcomers in Newport. Types we don't want around here. Let's pretend that I don't know you're all right, see? I'd say, "Mr. North, are you a flicker?"

THEOPHILUS. A what?

HENRY. A detective.

THEOPHILUS. I've never had anything to do with such things.

HENRY. I know that. I knew early you were no flicker. When I saw in the newspaper you were ready to teach Latin, that did it. There's no flicker ever been known that can handle Latin. You talk for a while.

THEOPHILUS. Well, I've got some ideas about the trees of Newport. And then there's my theory of "The Nine Cities of Newport."

HENRY. What's that?

THEOPHILUS. Well, I believe Newport may be like the old Trojan city, its treasures buried and unearthed—

HENRY. Stop right there. This is something Mrs. Cranston will want to hear.

THEOPHILUS. Who's Mrs. Cranston?

HENRY. Who's Mrs. Cranston?! Mate, if you don't know Mrs. Cranston, you don't know Newport. She's got a line on everything that happens here. You can bet you weren't in town for two hours before she knew you'd arrived.

THEOPHILUS. Is she a servant, too?

HENRY. Not any more. She was for much of her life. Climbed the ladder from scullery maid to upstairs maid to downstairs maid. But she has a fine place of her own now.

THEOPHILUS. And Mister Cranston?

HENRY. Who?

THEOPHILUS. If she was a maid, where did she get the money for her own place?

HENRY. What does that matter, Ted? It found its way to her. And every cook, valet, seamstress or doorman in Newport knows they can turn to her and be better for it. She wants to meet you. That's a very special honor, as she usually only likes to see servants in the house.

THEOPHILUS. But I am a servant, Henry!

HENRY. All these houses where you're gonna have students—you plan on going in through the front door?

THEOPHILUS. Well, yes, but—

HENRY. Then you're not a servant. She'll be very happy if I bring you to call. *(Hands THEOPHILUS a card)* Meet me at this address tonight, ten o'clock—unless that's past your bedtime.

(HENRY exits.)

THEOPHILUS. *(Out)* My spirits buoyed, I decide to treat

myself to a first-class lunch. I infiltrate the sanctum of the restaurant at the elite Muenchinger-King Hotel.

Scene 5
Myra, i

GEORGE. Mr. North?

THEOPHILUS. Yes.

GEORGE. My name is George Granberry. I should say George *Francis* Granberry because I have a cousin in town named George Herbert Granberry.

THEOPHILUS. Yes, Mr. Granberry.

GEORGE. I need your help. I'm told that you read aloud in English. English literature and all that.

THEOPHILUS. Yes, I do.

GEORGE. I'd like to discuss you reading aloud some books to my wife Myra. She's sort of an invalid this summer, and it would... kind of... help her pass the time.

THEOPHILUS. I see.

GEORGE. Mr. North, Myra is the brightest girl in the world. Quick as a whip. But when she was young she had teachers that were terrible bores; you know what schoolteachers are like. As a result of this she hates reading a book. Poetry, *The Three Musketeers*, Shakespeare...

(MYRA is revealed.)

MYRA. I just can't stand nonsense.

GEORGE. She's a very realistic girl. But she likes to be read to, for a while. I've tried to read aloud to her, and her nurse, Mrs. Cummings, does too, but after about ten minutes...

MYRA. Oh, stop. Let's talk instead.

(She goes.)

GEORGE. Mr. North, she's had two miscarriages. We're expecting a child again in about six months. The doctors have ordered her to spend all her afternoons on the sofa. I love Myra, but I can't spend all my afternoons just listening to her. Besides, I'm sort of an inventor. I have a laboratory in Middletown.

THEOPHILUS. An inventor, Mr. Granberry?

GEORGE. Oh, I tinker at some ideas I have. I keep it pretty secret. Mr. North, you may have to be a little patient with Myra at the beginning. She's strong-minded and very sincere. If you put her before a firing squad and asked her to name five plays by Shakespeare...

MYRA. *(Reappearing)* Go ahead and shoot.

GEORGE. She's got it against Shakespeare.

MYRA. He's piffle.

(She goes.)

GEORGE. She was born in Wisconsin and up there they don't allow anybody to tell them anything.

THEOPHILUS. I was born in Wisconsin.

GEORGE. *You were born in Wisconsin?*

THEOPHILUS. Yes.

GEORGE. You're a Badger!

THEOPHILUS. Yes.

GEORGE. Oh, that'll be a big recommendation. Myra's very proud of being a Badger. Well, do you think you could try it?

THEOPHILUS. All right, I'll try.

GEORGE. Thank you. *(More quietly.)* And you won't say a word about this to anyone?

THEOPHILUS. I make it a rule to never talk about my employers.

GEORGE. Well done. The thing is, we may meet at the house... or you may see me here with a "friend" of mine, a Miss Desmoulins. I'd appreciate it if you didn't mention it... in certain quarters—you see what I mean? Excuse me, Mr. North, I believe "my party" has just arrived; but I'm awfully glad that you're willing to give this reading a shot.

(He exits.)

THEOPHILUS. *(Out)* I return to the "Y" to construct a potential reading list personalized for Mrs. Granberry, have supper, then head out to meet Henry Simmons at the instructed address.

Scene 6
At Mrs. Cranston's, i

(WOMEN 1 and 2, MAN 3, and MRS. CRANSTON appear.)

WOMAN 1. Mrs. Cranston's: we are a large establishment
MAN 3. in the shadow of Trinity Church

WOMAN 2. consisting of three houses

WOMAN 1. built so close together

MAN 3. that it required merely making openings in the walls to unite us.

WOMAN 2. We are the unofficial hub of an indispensable section of Newport: the Servants' City.

WOMAN 1. A temporary boardinghouse for many servants

MAN 3. and a permanent residence for a few.

MRS. CRANSTON. But I do not run an employment agency.

WOMAN 2. Within our walls gossip is kept within bounds.

WOMAN 1. Mrs. Cranston says that it is unprofessional for hired help to discuss the private lives of those who feed them.

MRS. CRANSTON. But certain events may be alluded to... in confidence.

(The MAN and WOMEN go.)

HENRY. Mrs. Cranston, I should like you to make the acquaintance of my friend Teddie North.

THEOPHILUS. Theophilus, Ma'am.

MRS. CRANSTON. I'm very pleased, Mr. North.

THEOPHILUS. Thank you.

HENRY. He has only one fault as far as I can know, ma'am, he minds his own business.

MRS. CRANSTON. That recommends him to me, Mr. Simmons.

THEOPHILUS. I try not to get involved in situations beyond my control.

MRS. CRANSTON. Such as a marathon reading of the *Bible* to a certain eccentric's father, perhaps? *(To HENRY)* Mr. Simmons, you'll excuse me if I ask you to go into the bar for two minutes while I tell Mr. North something he should know.

HENRY. Yes, indeed, gracious lady.

(He exits.)

MRS. CRANSTON. Mr. North, as a young man who asserts himself, I feel you will most likely get involved in some situations "beyond your control" while you are here. If complications should present themselves to you, I hope you will get in touch with me, and that I may approach you if I hear a kettle boiling, as it were. Will you remember that?

THEOPHILUS. Thank you, Mrs. Cranston.

MRS. CRANSTON. Mr. Simmons, rejoin us and let us break the law a little bit. Please bring with you three gin-fizzes. Mr. North, there have been many rumors circulating regarding who you are.

HENRY. *(Returning)* Some think you're a scandal hound, Teddie. A newspaperman after dirt.

MRS. CRANSTON. During the season they're thick as flies. They are one element of a most dubious segment of Newport, filled with parasites, fortune-hunters and prying journalists.

HENRY. You were also suspected of being a "Jiggala!"

MRS. CRANSTON. Henry Simmons, you have your own language. The word is "gigolo."

HENRY. Thank you, ma'am. That's French for dancing partner with ambition. At first we thought you were one of them.

MRS. CRANSTON. Thank you, Henry.

HENRY. Nevertheless, Mrs. Cranston, we wouldn't think the worse of Mr. North here, if he found a sweet little thing in copper mines or railroads, would we?

MRS. CRANSTON. I advise against it, Mr. North.

THEOPHILUS. I have no intention of doing so, Mrs. Cranston. I believe that a keen mind can inoculate one against such pedestrian involvements. I hope to survey the world from a higher plane. But may I ask your reasons against it?

MRS. CRANSTON. I'll say no more. By the end of summer you'll have made your own observations.

HENRY. Mrs. Cranston, you should hear this idea Teddy's got about Newport.

MRS. CRANSTON. I would very much like to hear it.

THEOPHILUS. Well, one of my ambitions growing up was to be an archeologist. I was enthralled by Schliemann's discovery of ancient Troy—those nine cities one on top of the other. I think maybe Newport, Rhode Island has its own cities: variously beautiful, absurd, impressive, commonplace, all to be discovered by the simple turning of a stone.

HENRY. You're like a dictionary come to life, Teddy. Did you write that down somewhere?

MRS. CRANSTON. Mr. North, you may have the muse of a poet within you.

THEOPHILUS. No, Mrs. Cranston, I believe writing is a sedentary pursuit, and I long to see the world right now. But I have considered keeping a journal this summer...

MRS. CRANSTON. I propose a toast. To *you*, Mr. North.

THEOPHILUS. To *me*?

MRS. CRANSTON. You are a welcome surprise cast upon our shore.

THEOPHILUS. *(Out)* I am Gulliver, shipwrecked on the island of Aquidneck, and I could not have fallen on better luck.

Scene 7
The Fenwicks, ii

THEOPHILUS. *(Out)* Two days later Eloise approaches me at the end of my class.

ELOISE. Mr. North, I have a note from Mama. *(Giving it to him)* Aren't you going to read it?

THEOPHILUS. I'll wait. Just now I'd rather take you to the La Forge Tea Rooms for a hot fudge sundae. And perhaps every week—after I finish my lessons. Do you think this note engages or dismisses me?

ELOISE. *(Laughing)* I shan't tell you.

THEOPHILUS. You just have. You really do know a lot about what's going on, don't you?

ELOISE. Well, no one ever tells a young girl anything, so she has to be sort of a witch. She has to learn to read people's thoughts; she has to learn how to know things. Mr. North, I'm going to tell you a secret: Charles thinks he's an orphan, that he's adopted. That's what he thinks—that he's a prince from Poland or Hungary.

THEOPHILUS. Does he think that you're from royal birth, too?

ELOISE. I don't let him. Do you always tell the truth?

THEOPHILUS. I do to you. It's so boring to tell the truth to people who'd rather hear the other thing. Eloise, please read this letter to me, but don't ask me to explain it to you.

(He hands her the letter.)

ELOISE. "Dear Mr. North, Father Walsh says to tell you that

when he was young he had worked as a counselor in a boys'
camp, too. He told me to tell you to go ahead. It comforts me to
think of our composer from Salzburg. Sincerely, Millicent Fenwick." *(Handing him back the letter.)* Thank you. Wasn't Mozart
from Salzburg?

THEOPHILUS. Is it hard to be a witch, Eloise? Does it make
living harder?

ELOISE. No! It keeps you so busy. You have to be on your
toes. It keeps you from going stale.

THEOPHILUS. Oh, is that one of your worries?

ELOISE. Isn't it everybody's?

(She goes.)

Scene 8
Myra, ii

THEOPHILUS. *(Out)* On the appointed afternoon I wheel
up to the door of George and Myra Granberry's home, Sea
Ledges.

(MAN 2 appears.)

MAN 2. I am Sea Ledges; a vestige from the city of Newport's Empire Builders. They once erected their castles here, having suddenly awakened to the realization that inland New York is
crushingly hot in summer. With them came fashion, display and
ornate façade. I get the name Sea Ledges from my vast lawn and

gardens which gently slope to a low cliff above the ocean.

(He goes.)

THEOPHILUS. *(Out)* I am led to Mrs. Granberry's "afternoon room," the placid grace of a woman with child awaiting me, within. *(MYRA and MRS. CUMMINGS are revealed.)* Good afternoon, Mrs. Granberry. I am Theophilus North. Mr. Granberry has engaged me to read aloud to you. *(Long pause as she gazes at him in astonishment and rage.)* Will you kindly introduce me to your companion?

MYRA. Mrs. Cummings, Mr. North.

THEOPHILUS. Are you from Wisconsin, like Mrs. Granberry and me?

MRS. CUMMINGS. Oh, no, sir. I'm from Boston.

THEOPHILUS. Are you also fond of reading?

MRS. CUMMINGS. Oh, I love reading, but I don't get much time for it, you know.

THEOPHILUS. Surely some of your patients like a bit of reading? Something light and amusing?

MRS. CUMMINGS. We have to be careful, sir. When I was in training the Mother Directress told us that she had once read *Mrs. Wiggs of the Cabbage Patch* to a surgical case. They had to restitch him.

THEOPHILUS. It's a lovely book. Ladies, we certainly don't want to read anything that's boring, do we? So I suggest we draw up some rules.

MYRA. What kind of rules?

THEOPHILUS. I suggest that I start reading a book and that you let me read it for a quarter of an hour without interruption. Then you give me a sign that I may go on for another quarter of

an hour, or to start some other book. Does that seem reasonable
to you, ma'am?

MYRA. Don't call me "ma'am." Let me make it clear to
you, Mr. West, that there's something behind all this that I don't
like. I don't like being treated as an idiot child.

THEOPHILUS. *(Rising)* Oh, then there's been some misun-
derstanding. I'll say good afternoon. Mrs. Cummings, I hope I
may meet you at another time. Please recall me as Mr. North, not
Mr. West.

MYRA. *(Sharply)* Mr. North, it's not your fault that I don't
like the whole idea. You've been asked to come here and read to
me, so please sit down and begin.

THEOPHILUS. Thank you, Mrs. Granberry. *(He opens a
book.)* This is *Daisy Miller.* It was written by a man who lived in
Newport when he was young. Not far from this house.

MYRA. Then why did he write books?

THEOPHILUS. I beg your pardon?

MYRA. If he was so rich why did he take the trouble to write
books? Was he feeble-minded?

THEOPHILUS. *(Slowly)* No, I think he got tired of buying
and selling railroads, and building hotels and naming them after
his family. So he wrote it all down—how people behave in the
world, the happy and the unhappy. When he died, his last book—
still unfinished on his desk—was a novel laid in Newport, called
The Ivory Tower, about the emptiness and waste of life here.

MYRA. Mr. North, are you trying to make me look ridiculous?

THEOPHILUS. No, ma'am.

MYRA. What do you mean "emptiness and waste of life?"

THEOPHILUS. Those were not my words. I was reporting
what Henry James said.

MYRA. In Wisconsin we don't quibble. You said it and you meant it.

THEOPHILUS. I don't know Newport life well enough to make any judgment about it. I come and go on a bicycle.

MYRA. Don't contradict a pregnant woman. Stop running away from my questions.

THEOPHILUS. Mrs. Granberry—

MYRA. Don't call me "ma'am" and don't call me "Mrs. Granberry!" Call me Myra!

THEOPHILUS. Mrs. Granberry, I make it a rule that in all—

MYRA. *We're from Wisconsin.* Don't be such an *Easterner.*

MRS. CUMMINGS. Oh, Mr. North, I wish you would make an exception in this case, seeing that... you're both Badgers.

MYRA. You and your rules. Very well, I'll forget the "emptiness of life" comment if I can make a rule, too: after the first forty-five minutes we take half an hour to talk.

THEOPHILUS. As you wish.

MYRA. You may begin.

THEOPHILUS. *Daisy Miller. (Out)* After exactly forty-five minutes—

MYRA. Time! Theophilus, tell us about your life here—your friends, enemies, good times, and if you're making any money.

THEOPHILUS. I would much rather an account of those things in your life.

MYRA. *(With consideration)* Well, I grow older. I wait for my baby. I eat breakfast. Then the doctor calls and asks if I've been good. He gets ten dollars for that. If it's a sunny day Cora and I go to Bailey's Beach. We sit well wrapped up in a corner so as not to have to talk to people, and we watch the old boots and orange crates drift by. My father was the richest man in Wisconsin. He owned hundreds of lakes, and if any one of them was as dirty as Bailey's Beach, he'd drain it and plant it with trees. What else do I do, Cora?

MRS. CUMMINGS. You go to luncheon parties, Mrs. Granberry.

MYRA. Yes, I do. Ladies. Men there only on Sundays. All named Granberry. I come home early and rest and I can't think of anything else to tell you. *(To MRS. CUMMINGS)* Cora, do you know if Mr. Granberry is home yet?

MRS. CUMMINGS. No, I don't believe so, ma'am.

MYRA. Oh. Mr. North, that will be all for today, I think. Leave that here and bring some others next time. It's starting a book that kills me. I'll finish that on my own.

Scene 9
The Fenwicks, iii

THEOPHILUS. *(Out)* I now have a plan in mind for my meetings with Charles: the lessons will contain the day's grammatical problem and a "dynamite word:" coucher, *derriere*... All lessons are conducted in French, which, for the most part, will be translated here. But now and then, we'll test your skills. *(To CHARLES, entering)* Bonjour, Charles. It's a lovely day. How are you today?

CHARLES. Fine.

THEOPHILUS. What a handsome sweater. Where did you find such a handsome sweater?

CHARLES. Gift.

THEOPHILUS. *(Pause)* Charles, today we're going to work with the second person singular "tu," which is used with children, your very old friends, and your family. Of course, lovers call each other "tu"; all conversations in bed are in the second person singular. *(Charles reacts.)* Charles, what are those odd-looking kiosks in the streets of Paris called—those constructions for the convenience of men only? *(Pause)* Charles?

CHARLES. Pissoirs!

THEOPHILUS. Yes. *(Out)* It took him ten minutes to recover from that.

CHARLES. Monsieur North, my mother would like to invite you to an informal supper with the family on Sunday.

THEOPHILUS. Yes, that sounds— Actually, no. That is very kind of your mother, but I make a rule not to accept invitations from any employers. It's very hard to refuse this kindness from so remarkable a mother. I hope you are finding a hundred delicate ways of expressing your admiration to her, as all French sons do, and—I'm sorry to say—all American sons don't. You do, don't you, Charles?

CHARLES. Oui... oui, monsieur le professeur.

(He goes.)

THEOPHILUS. *(Out)* There is still much work to be done. Back at the desk of the "Y," a telephone message is given to me:

SARAH BOSWORTH. *(Appearing; out)* From Mrs. Sarah McHenry Bosworth. *(Aside.)* Privilege, privilege.... Mr. North: it is a fortunate occurrence for you that the position of personal reader to my father is still available. Nine Gables awaits your call.

THEOPHILUS. *(Out)* Very well, Fate, I place myself in your

hands. So next on my dance card will be Mrs. "Privilege-
Privilege" Bosworth, and her father. At the library I retrieve *Notable Families of Eastern Society, 1925,* and with it ride to my
appointment.

(He gets on his bike with book open.)

Scene 10
Nine Gables, i

THEOPHILUS. "The Honorable Dr. James McHenry Bosworth:..."

(DR. BOSWORTH is revealed.)

DR. BOSWORTH. *(Out)* "74, widower, father of six and
grandfather of... many. Has served as attaché and ambassador to
several countries on three continents. Lives in Newport year-
round and several of his children have homes in the vicinity. Mrs.
Sarah McHenry Bosworth is his daughter." *(Whispering)* She's
divorced.
SARAH. *(Out)* I have no children, and have resumed my
maiden name.

(SARAH and DR. BOSWORTH go.)

THEOPHILUS. *(Out)* Friday morning is radiant. Has each

Friday been like this? Have I noticed? I ride my bicycle under the grand entrance arch and up the improbably lengthy drive towards the front door.

(WOMAN 1 appears.)

WOMAN 1. Nine Gables. I am a long rambling cottage. Weather-silvered shingles, wide verandas, turrets and gables from which you can see the beacons of six lighthouses at night. I am an example of nineteenth-century intellectual Newport; families from Cambridge, professors from Harvard, philosophers and novelists. Through my latched screen door on any given day you can see a platoon of servants polishing floors, and dusting the books of one of the greatest private libraries in America.

(WOMAN 1 goes. THEOPHILUS rings the bell. A butler, WILLIS, opens the door.)

THEOPHILUS. Mr. North to see Mrs. Bosworth.

WILLIS. In general, sir, this door is not used in the morning. You will find the garden door around the corner of the house at your left.

(He shuts the door. THEOPHILUS rings the bell again. WILLIS answers.)

THEOPHILUS. Mrs. Bosworth asked me to call at this address.

WILLIS. *This* door is not generally used.

(He shuts the door. THEOPHILUS rings the bell again. WILLIS

answers.)

THEOPHILUS. Thank you, Mr. Fezziwig. I assume that you are expecting the piano tuner?

WILLIS. What?

THEOPHILUS. Or the chiropodist. What a lovely day, Mr. Fezziwig. Kindly tell Mrs. Bosworth that I have called.

WILLIS. My name is not Fe—Sir, take your bicycle to the door I have indicated.

THEOPHILUS. I knew Dr. Bosworth well in Singapore. Raffles Hotel, you know. We used to play fan-tan.

WILLIS. What? I refuse to be engaged any further in this ridiculous twaddle.

THEOPHILUS. Temple bells and all that. Punkahs swaying from the ceiling—

WILLIS. I've had enough of you. I am shutting the door again. Deranged. Positively!

THEOPHILUS. When the Queen arrives, please remind her she still has the ice tongs I loaned her.

WILLS. Demented scalawag, go away before I am forced to call the authorities!

(Enter SARAH BOSWORTH.)

SARAH. And what is going on out here?

THEOPHILUS. *(Out)* Mrs. Bosworth is the type of person who enjoys beginning sentences with the word "and."

SARAH. And who are you?

THEOPHILUS. Theophilus North.

SARAH. I am expecting you for *some* time, Mr. North. Follow me into my sitting room.

THEOPHILUS. *(To WILLIS)* Thank you for your help.

SARAH. I am Mrs. Bosworth, Dr. Bosworth's eldest daughter. I do not know what caused that commotion, nor do I want to. You will sit down, please.

THEOPHILUS. Thank you, but I prefer—

SARAH. Sit. My father's eyes tire easily. His readers have proved unsatisfactory. I know his tastes. As I mentioned some time ago, he has a strong interest in philosophy and also the *Bible*, which he would like to have read to him in its entirety.

THEOPHILUS. I see. At my rate that would be a considerable sum of money.

SARAH. Yes, I would like to know if you are able to make special reduced terms for such a reading.

THEOPHILUS. I could read the Old Testament in Hebrew. There are no vowels in Hebrew. That would reduce the time by about seven hours.

SARAH. But he wouldn't understand it.

THEOPHILUS. What has understanding got to do with it? He's already read it eleven times.

SARAH. Perhaps we should focus on Philosophy.

THEOPHILUS. I'll offer you a budget plan and read it in Aramaic. Very terse, very condensed.

SARAH. Thank you, Mr. North. *(She lowers her voice.)* I am sorry to have to tell you that my father finds readers with conviction such as yours very tiring. I don't think you should waste your time any longer.

DR. BOSWORTH. *(Off)* Sarah! Sarah!

(WILLIS appears.)

SARAH. *(Holding out her hand)* Thank you, Mr. North.

Good morning.

DR.. BOSWORTH. *(Off)* Sarah!

SARAH. Willis, go about your work, this is none of your affair!

(WILLIS exits. DR. BOSWORTH enters.)

DR. BOSWORTH. Let me see that young man, Sarah. Finally we have found someone with resonance! God help us, the only readers you've ever found are retired librarians with mice in their throats.

SARAH. Father, you *will* see Mr. North directly. Go back to your desk at once. You mustn't get agitated. *(He exits.)* For the second time in fifteen minutes, Mr. North, you have introduced discord into Nine Gables. You really must change your ways. In the event that Dr. Bosworth approves of you as a reader, there are some things you should know. My father is not well. He is easily excitable, and prone to occasional... flights of fancy. Any encouragement from you over such things will only lead to difficulty.

DR. BOSWORTH. *(Off)* Sarah!

SARAH. I want you to remember what I've said. Have you heard me?

THEOPHILUS. Thank you, Mrs. Bosworth.

SARAH. Any further trouble from you and you go out of this house at once. *(Calling him in as she exits)* Father, this is Mr. North.

DR. BOSWORTH. Please sit down, Mr. North. I am Dr. Bosworth.

THEOPHILUS. Indeed, I know of your distinguished career, Dr. Bosworth.

DR. BOSWORTH. Very good. Where were you born?

THEOPHILUS. Madison, Wisconsin.

DR. BOSWORTH. What was your father's occupation?

THEOPHILUS. He owned and operated a newspaper.

DR. BOSWORTH. How many languages do you speak?

THEOPHILUS. I speak—

DR. BOSWORTH. What have you done since leaving school? What are your plans? How much money do you make? Do you get enough to eat?

THEOPHILUS. *(Standing)* Dr. Bosworth, I was told that you have had many unsatisfactory readers. I foresee that I shall disappoint you also. Good morning.

DR. BOSWORTH. What? What?

THEOPHILUS. *(Exiting)* Good morning, sir.

DR. BOSWORTH. Mr. North! Kindly let me explain myself. *(THEOPHILUS re-enters.)* Please sit down, sir. I did not mean to be intrusive. I have not left this house for seven years except to visit the hospital. We who are shut in develop an excessive curiosity about those who attend us. Will you accept my apology?

THEOPHILUS. Yes, sir. Thank you.

DR. BOSWORTH. Thank you... Are you free to read to me until twelve-thirty?

THEOPHILUS. I am.

DR. BOSWORTH. Good. I have a first edition philosophy by George Berkeley here. Perhaps that's a good place to start.

THEOPHILUS. Very well, Dr. Bosworth.

DR. BOSWORTH. By the way, young man, that Getting-Up-and-Leaving-the-Room trick is very effective, isn't it? I did it to William McKinley all the time. Read the inscription.

THEOPHILUS. *(Taken off guard)* What?

DR. BOSWORTH. The Berkeley, read the inscription.

THEOPHILUS. Yes. "From George Berkeley, To my esteemed friend, Dean Jonathan... Swift." *(He looks at DR. BOSWORTH and they both begin to laugh.)* Dr. Bosworth, it will take me some time to recover from my astonishment over holding this book.

DR. BOSWORTH. I know! I know! You are aware that Berkeley lived three years in Newport? A glorious cottage called "Whitehall," where they say at night the groaning of the tree branches in the wind tells secrets of the universe. My plans have been to— *(Whispering.)* Mr. North, I do believe this house has ears. Will you climb up on the chair and see if there's some kind of listening devise hidden in the lighting fixture?

THEOPHILUS. No, Dr. Bosworth. I was engaged as a reader, not an electrical engineer.

DR. BOSWORTH. Good choice. Edison once asked me if I knew anything about electricity. I lied and said "yes." Want to see the scar?

THEOPHILUS. Perhaps later.

DR. BOSWORTH. Time! Time! They tell me I am not well. Sh! *(Whispering)* We must not discuss this any more.

(He goes.)

Scene 11
The Fenwicks, iv

THEOPHILUS. *(Out)* And so from avoiding a topic in one place, to actively pursuing one in another... *(To CHARLES)* Bonjour, Charles.

CHARLES. Bonjour, monsieur le professeur.

THEOPHILUS. Charles, you've been in Paris. After dark you must have seen certain women addressing gentlemen in a low voice from doorways and alleys. What do they usually say? *(Out)* The scarlet flag is high on the mast. I can wait.

CHARLES. Voulez-vous coucher avec moi?

THEOPHILUS. Good. Charles, you're sitting alone at a bar and one of these petites dames slides up beside you. "Tu veux m'offrir un verre de champagne?" How do you answer, Charles? I'm waiting...

CHARLES. Non, mademoiselle... merci.... Pas ce soir.

THEOPHILUS. Très bien, Charles! Could you make it a little more easy and charming? In France there is universal respect for women of every age and at every level of society, even when she's a prostitute. I have an idea. I'm going to pretend I'm one of those girls. You are strolling behind the Paris Opera. I think this will be good! *(Out)* I hope this doesn't damage him. *(CHARLES stands petrified.)* Come on, Charles. It's a play, not a cage of tigers. Bonsoir, mon chou.

CHARLES. Bonsoir, mademoiselle.

THEOPHILUS. Tu es seul? Want a little amusement?

CHARLES. Je suis occupé ce soir...Merci. Perhaps another time. Tu es charmante.

THEOPHILUS. Ooo! Mais, cheri, I have a lovely room!

CHARLES. How do I get out of this?

THEOPHILUS. I suggest you make your departure quick, but cordial.

CHARLES. Mademoiselle, je suis en retard. J'ai besoin de partir. Mais au revoir. *(He pats THEOPHILUS's elbow.)* Bonne chance, chère amie.

THEOPHILUS. Magnifique, Charles! Magnifique! *(Out)* On days when the lessons begin with heavy dynamite, Charles is quick. He laughs; he skates over depth bombs; he uses his own past in stories—

CHARLES. *(Out)* And my complexion is clearing up.

Scene 12
Myra, iii

THEOPHILUS. *(Out)* As for Myra, by now we have also read the openings of *Ethann Frome, Jane Eyre, The Scarlet Letter,* and *Tom Jones.*

MRS. CUMMINGS. Oh, Mr. North, she reads all the time. She'll ruin her eyes.

THEOPHILUS. But you never learn how the stories turn out.

MRS. CUMMINGS. She tells me, sir; it's as good as a moving-picture! Jane Eyre! Oh, what happened to her!

MYRA. All right, back to the books.

THEOPHILUS. What did you think of *The Scarlet Letter*?

MYRA. I don't know. She should've just torn the thing off and moved to Chicago.

THEOPHILUS. And what else?

MYRA. You wouldn't understand. They're all so new to me, those lives and people doing things. Sometimes they're more real than life. What were your feelings about the books, when you first read them?

THEOPHILUS. Well, I thought that many of—

MYRA. I didn't ask what you *thought*, Theophilus, I asked what you *felt*. It's always the same with you: rules and thoughts. I'd go mad.

(There is knock. Enter GEORGE GRANBERRY.)

GEORGE. How's my little squirrel today?

MYRA. *(Coming alive.)* Very well, thank you.

GEORGE. Excellent. *(Starting to exit.)* Well, then, I'll just—

MYRA. George, I want you to buy all the books I've read. Mr. North has to go and get them at the People's Library. They're not very clean and people have written silly things in the margins. I want my own books, so that I can write my own silly things in the margins.

GEORGE. All right, Myra.

MYRA. I'm a little tired and I think I'll ask Mr. North to cancel the reading today. But we'll pay him just the same. But don't you go, George. Please.

Scene 13
Nine Gables, ii

THEOPHILUS. *(Out)* Back at Nine Gables, Berkeley and Leibniz, Halley and Swift surround me in the great study, which seems the heart of nineteenth-century Newport.

DR. BOSWORTH. Come here quickly, Mr. North! Something astonishing!

THEOPHILUS. What, Dr. Bosworth?

DR. BOSWORTH. At our last meeting Isaac Newton was mocking dear Berkeley's doctrines of Christianity.

THEOPHILUS. Yes?

DR. BOSWORTH. Read how Berkeley responds to him in *The Analyst.*

(DR. BOSWORTH hands THEOPHILUS a book.)

THEOPHILUS. "Newton's fluxions are obscure—"

DR. BOSWORTH. Take that!

THEOPHILUS. "Repugnant and precarious—"

DR. BOSWORTH. Smashed! Demolished!

THEOPHILUS. "They are neither finite... nor yet nothing."

DR. BOSWORTH. That's our boy! Pulverize him! I must dance to Berkeley! *(He dances. A jig?)* I also have a great respect for Garibaldi. Tomorrow we must dress like Italians to honor him.

THEOPHILUS. I'll wear a pork-pie hat.

DR. BOSWORTH. Perfect! Bless my heart, Mr. North, it is *nice* to have a young man around who appreciates these things. My daughter couldn't be less interested.

SARAH. *(Offstage)* Father! Are you dancing in there?!
DR. BOSWORTH. She used to love to dance....

(DR. BOSWORTH exits; CHARLES appears.)

Scene 14
The Fenwicks, v

THEOPHILUS. Bonjour, Charles.
CHARLES. Mr. North, I have an idea! May we do another play?
THEOPHILUS. Absolument, Charles. Who are you?
CHARLES. The King of France!
THEOPHILUS. Very good. But let us say that you are the King of France, who in modern times is not permitted to use that title or wear the crown. He is called the Prétendant, "the Pretender." We'll set it in a great restaurant of Paris, of which I am the proprietor, Monsieur Véfour. Now... vous entrez!

(CHARLES enters, hands imaginary cape and top hat to THEOPHILUS.)

CHARLES. *(With some arrogance)* Bonsoir, Monsieur Véfour.
THEOPHILUS. Charles, just a moment. The French have a word for cold, condescending self-importance: morgue. You would be horrified if you thought your subjects attributed that quality to you.

CHARLES. Of course! Let's start over. Monsieur le professeur... can we ask Eloise to see it? She's sitting right over there.

THEOPHILUS. Yes, indeed! Let's invite her. *(Calling off.)* Eloise, we're doing a little one-act play. Would you like to be our audience?

ELOISE. *(Entering.)* Bien sûr, Monsieur le professeur!

THEOPHILUS. Give it the works, Charles!

(CHARLES enters, smiling. Hands imaginary cape and top hat to THEOPHILUS, as coat-check girl.)

CHARLES. Bonsoir, mademoiselle. Tout va bien?

THEOPHILUS. *(Curtsying)* Bonsoir, Monseigneur. Votre Altesse nous fait un très grand honneur.

CHARLES. Ah, Henri-Paul, comment allez-vous?

THEOPHILUS. *(As Véfour)* Très bien, Monseigneur, merci.

CHARLES. Et madame votre femme, comment va-t-elle?

THEOPHILUS. Très bien, Monseigneur, elle vous remercie.

CHARLES. Et les chère enfants?

THEOPHILUS. Très bien, Monseigneur, merci.

CHARLES. Tiens! C'est votre fils? *(As to a child)* Comment vous appelez-vous, monsieur? Frédéric? Comme votre grand-père. Mon grand-père aimait bien votre grand-père. *(To Véfour)* Dites, Henri-Paul, j'ai démandé des couverts pour trois personnes. Ça vous gênerait beaucoup?

THEOPHILUS. Pas du tout, Monseigneur. Si Votre Altesse aura la bonté de me suivre.

CHARLES. Henri-Paul, c'est très bien de rentrer dans ces parts. Connaîssiez-vous, mon ami, que ma mère m'apportait ici pour le première fois quand j'avais douze ans?

THEOPHILUS. Vraiment?

CHARLES. Absolument! Nous avons mangé ici tout les Di-
manches depuis longtemps. Oh-la-la ma mère. C'est vrai que t'as
créé une dessert dans son nom?

THEOPHILUS. Oui, c'est ça.

CHARLES. J'espère que ça contient beaucoup de sucre et de
crème! Mais je suis en retard et mes invités m'attendent. *(To
Eloise.)* Mon Dieu! C'est vrai? C'est possible? Ah, Madame la
Marquise... chère cousine!

ELOISE. *(Deep curtsy)* Mon Prince!

(He raises her up and kisses her hand.)

CHARLES. Mes amis, les rues sont si bondées; c'est la fin
du monde. Quelquefois nous nous sentons...affamé. Mais ici tous
la carte est toujours remplie. Le banquet nous attend!

*(ELOISE is wide-eyed in wonder. She throws her arms around
her brother and kisses him with poignant intensity.)*

THEOPHILUS. Charles, you have surpassed yourself. I will
arrange with the Newport French Academy to give you the ex-
amination for those who have completed three years of French.
I'm sure you'll pass it splendidly and our lessons will have been a
resounding success.

CHARLES. It's over!?

THEOPHILUS. Yes. Now you must give your time to
American history and algebra.

CHARLES. Oui. Merci, monsieur le professeur.

(He shakes THEOPHILUS's hand and exits.)

ELOISE. Mr. North, your play was lovely. Will you write one for me?

THEOPHILUS. No, Eloise. Such things are not for me. But I will meet you on Friday for our visit to the tea room.

(She goes as MYRA appears.)

Scene 15
Myra, iv

THEOPHILUS. Good afternoon, Myra. Where is Mrs. Cummings?

MYRA. I've asked her to wait on the balcony for a few minutes so I can discuss something with you in private.

THEOPHILUS. That might jeopardize both our positions, Myra. What is it?

MYRA. Do you know a woman named Desmoulins?

THEOPHILUS. I have heard her name in passing conversations and seen her once, but have never had occasion to meet her.

MYRA. Is she a harlot and a strumpet and that other thing in *Tom Jones*?

THEOPHILUS. No, indeed. I understand she is a woman of some refinement. She is what some people would call an "emancipated" woman.

MYRA. "Emancipate" means to free the slaves. Was she a slave?

THEOPHILUS. No. Stop this nonsense and tell me what

you're trying to get at.

    MYRA. Is she better looking than I am?

    THEOPHILUS. No.

    MYRA. Badger?

    THEOPHILUS. Badger.

    MYRA. BADGER?

    THEOPHILUS. BADGER! I'll go call Mrs. Cummings.

    MYRA. Stop! Have you had dinner every Wednesday night with my husband and Miss Desmoulins at the Muenchinger-King?

    THEOPHILUS. *Never.* Please get to the point.

    MYRA. I have received two anonymous letters.

    THEOPHILUS. Myra! You tore them up at once.

    MYRA. No.

(She pulls them from out of her book.)

    THEOPHILUS. I'm ashamed of you. We are surrounded in this world by people filled with hate and envy and nastiness. You should have torn them to bits, unread, and put them out of your mind.

    MYRA. They say you had dinner.

    THEOPHILUS. That's just a sample of the lies that fill anonymous letters.

(MYRA bursts into tears.)

    MYRA. But, Theophilus, maybe they're right. Maybe my husband loves Miss Desmoulins. Maybe my baby has no father any more. Then I might as well die, because I love my husband more than anything else in the world.

THEOPHILUS. Myra, no Badger cries after the age of eleven.

MYRA. I'm sorry.

THEOPHILUS. They fight. They're smart, they're brave and they defend what they've got. Now put this whole wretched business out of your head. Badgers always catch the snake. *(Calling her in.)* Mrs. Cummings, it's school time. Mrs. Granberry heard an ugly bit of gossip. I told her that no one who's intelligent and beautiful and rich has ever escaped gossip. Aren't I right?

MRS. CUMMINGS. Oh, Mr. North, you're very right.

THEOPHILUS. Today we are going to try something new: *Twelfth Night* and *As You Like It.*

MYRA. Oh, Theophilus! Not Shakespeare! *Please!* His plays are so childish. All those girls dressing up in men's clothes. It's idiotic!

THEOPHILUS. But they have to do it because their backs are up against the wall. What girls they are: intelligent, resourceful. They face even the biggest catastrophe with bravery and humor. Don't you think there's something in that, Mrs. Cummings?

MRS. CUMMINGS. Oh, Mr. North, I think that's why nurses laugh so much when they're off duty. It helps us... to survive. Mrs. Granberry, can't we please ask Mr. North to read to us a little out of Shakespeare?

MYRA. Well... if it's not too long.

THEOPHILUS. My idea was that we all take parts.

MRS. CUMMINGS. Oh! I can't read poetry-English. I couldn't do that. You'll have to excuse me.

MYRA. Cora, if that's how Mr. North wants it, I suppose we must let him have his way.

THEOPHILUS. Now speak slowly, everybody—*slowly.*

MRS. CUMMINGS. *(Reading, slowly)* "If music be the food

of love, play on."

THEOPHILUS. *(Out)* Within the week we have done scenes from those plays, repeating them and switching roles, the balcony scene from *Romeo and Juliet,* and the trial scene from *The Merchant of Venice.*

MRS. CUMMINGS. *(Out)* I astonish myself as Shylock. But it is Mrs. Granberry who says, at the end of every scene,

MYRA. Let's do it again! Out on the balcony!

(She and MRS. CUMMINGS exit.)

Scene 16
The Fenwicks, vi

THEOPHILUS. *(Out)* As promised, I meet Eloise for our weekly sundae. This time, she is dressed all in white.

ELOISE. I'll have tea this morning. Last night there were no guests. At table Charles brushed away Mario and held the chair for Mother. He kissed her on the forehead. And he told a joke! When he sat down Papa said, "How is your tennis, son?" And Charles said, "Fine, Papa," and gave a quote from Tennyson!

THEOPHILUS. Eloise!

ELOISE. You grown-ups suddenly woke up about Charles. You saw he was all caught up in a sort of spider's web; he was afraid of everything.

THEOPHILUS. Eloise, if you see that Charles has cut his way out of that spider's web, you can tell yourself that it's all due to you.

ELOISE. No it isn't. I just think that when you love someone, you remember who they really are. So if they get afraid, and
forget, you help scare away dragons until they remember, too.

THEOPHILUS. I do so enjoy our visits, Eloise. You give me
such an interesting perspective on the world.

ELOISE. Mr. North, this is the last time we'll meet here.

THEOPHILUS. But why?

ELOISE. I shan't tell you that now, Mr. North. A girl my age
has to retain some mystery, you know.

THEOPHILUS. I should hardly think that is a problem with
you, Eloise. But I do hope our paths will cross again.

ELOISE. Perhaps they shall.

THEOPHILUS. Eloise?

ELOISE. Yes.

THEOPHILUS. What quote from Tennyson did Charles
give?

(As she whispers it in his ear, CHARLES appears.)

CHARLES. "I am a part of all that I have seen."

*(THEOPHILUS is stunned. He views MRS. FENWICK and her
children as they form a tableau, then are gone.)*

THEOPHILUS. *(Out)* "A part of all that I have seen?" What
have I seen? Nothing! What the hell am I still doing here? With
all my ambitions, what am I? I am a free man, accountable to no
one, who measures his life in nods and shrugs and forty-five minute increments. A free man, who watches his time pass on strangers' clocks on foreign mantels. A free man whose life swims by

as I sit and read other people's stories, my journals filled with insignificant notes about melted sundaes and drifting boots! I was meant to see the world! Greek ruins, great walls! If a man travels enough he'll run into amazing places, great people and excitement. Isn't there someplace I should be?

There is a spot in Newport, on the southernmost tip of Aquidneck Island. On this spot stands the Brenton Point Lighthouse. Perhaps because of the small rocky bluff on which it stands, or perhaps because it is the last piece of land before the vast Atlantic, the winds surrounding this lighthouse are unique. The seagulls know it and gather by the hundreds. They need merely to spread their wings and they are carried skyward with no effort on their part; they levitate before your eyes as you stand on the viewing deck, lifted towards the heavens. Oh, how the winds blow. Around the lighthouse, over the sea grass, above the scattered boats and sea bathers, and off! I've got to get out of here—now. Kindnesses have been show to me, which perhaps one day I can repay. But now I must collect my things at the Y. By morning I'll be gone. By noon I'll be well on my way to... to...

BILL. *(Entering.)* Theophilus? Theophilus?!

THEOPHILUS. Yes, Bill.

BILL. I need your help.

THEOPHILUS. I'm sorry, Bill, but I—

BILL. A problem has been dropped in my lap. Probably my job is at stake. I'm asking you to help me, Theophilus... as a friend.

THEOPHILUS. *(Out)* Damn.

(Blackout.)

End of Act I

ACT II

Scene 1

THEOPHILUS. *(Out)* Yes, I'm still here. And so are you. How can I say "no" to a man who entreats my help so earnestly? Cairo, St. Petersburg and Sydney will most likely stand until next week. But as soon as this job is done I am on my way to the lands of the living and astounding sites.

(BILL WENTWORTH enters.)

BILL. Theophilus, a problem has been dropped in my lap. I need your help on a little expedition that's not in the regular run of things—if you're willing.

THEOPHILUS. If it would be of any service to you, Bill, send me to the North Pole.

BILL. That might attract attention. This is what they call a "confidential mission." The chairman of our Board of Governors here is a Mr. Augustus Bell. His older daughter Diana is about twenty-six. It seems that Mr. Bell has a personal family issue involving his daughter which he wishes me to resolve: In two days, Diana is going to try and elope. It's very difficult to deal with the rich, Theophilus. Mr. Bell thinks it's my obvious duty to drop everything and assist him. I will not do it. But I told him I knew someone who was level-headed and resourceful. I didn't tell him your name, but I told him you were a Yale man. He's a

Yale man, too. Can you help?
    THEOPHILUS. When can I meet him?

(Shift to MRS. CRANSTON's begins.)

    BILL. Day after tomorrow, nine o'clock, in my office. Thanks, Theophilus.

Scene 2
At Mrs. Cranston's, ii

    MRS. CRANSTON. A prominent, wealthy father who is difficult, with a daughter who wants to elope. Well, that narrows it down to about fifteen families.

    HENRY. If Bill Wentworth asked you to help, I'd lay good odds that it's——

    MRS. CRANSTON. No names, Henry! Rules of the house!

    HENRY. Of course. Sorry, ma'am.

    MRS. CRANSTON. That's all right, Henry. Do you know what you're going to do, Theophilus?

    THEOPHILUS. Not in the least, Mrs. Cranston. But that's why I am actually looking forward to it. I will have to rely on my wits. At last, a real adventure!

    HENRY. I feel for the poor bloke who got stymied into taking her. Some of those girls can be awful difficult.

    THEOPHILUS. How do you mean, Henry?

    HENRY. Seems pretty clear to me that the partner who owns

the money owns the whip.

MRS. CRANSTON. Well said, Henry. And a girl brought up with great wealth thinks she has great brains, too. As for the father, the only thing to do with a man like that is to continue looking at him expectantly, as though eventually he were going to say something convincing.

HENRY. Without agreement and applause, he'll just gasp for air and deflate.

THEOPHILUS. Thank you both. I'll be certain to remember that. I need to learn all I can about being a Rascal. I don't think I've fared too well so far.

MRS. CRANSTON. But the French sounds as if it went smashingly. And the Shakespeare seems most promising.

THEOPHILUS. Yes, but I think I've gone about it in the wrong way. I've almost allowed myself to, how shall I say, "invest the situations of the parties with a personal regard." I think that must be the first rule of a Rascal: don't care... too much.

MRS. CRANSTON. Perhaps there is something in that, Theophilus. Perhaps. But we should let you go. You have a big day coming.

(She and HENRY go.)

THEOPHILUS. Indeed. Adventure! *(Out)* Back at the "Y" a visitor is waiting for me.

Scene 3
At the "Y"

SARAH BOSWORTH. *(Entering)* Mr. North.

THEOPHILUS. Mrs. Bosworth.

SARAH. I have called to inform you of your unfortunate loss. The position of personal reader to my father has been filled with someone else. You need not take your valuable time visiting Nine Gables again.

THEOPHILUS. I thank you for your thoughtful advisement, Mrs. Bosworth. In mourning for my loss I will schedule twenty-five minutes of insomnia this evening.

SARAH. Good afternoon.

THEOPHILUS. And Mrs. Bosworth—? May I request that should you feel the need to contact me again, you do so in writing? This *is* a Christian organization, and I believe people have begun to whisper about us.

(She exits.)

Scene 4
Diana Bell

THEOPHILUS. *(Out)* The next day I awake early, unable to sleep at the prospect of adventure. My mounting excitement inspires me to find a new route to Bill's office. An impulsive right turn brings a wonderful discovery.

MAN 2. *(Appearing)* I am a glorious section of Newport,

which contains some of the most beautiful edifices in America: Newport as an eighteenth-century town. It was from this very town that Rochambeau and Washington launched a sea campaign that successfully turned the course of a war. The War for Independence.

(He goes.)

THEOPHILUS. *(Out)* At nine a.m. I arrive at Bill's office, armed with some sound advice. *(To BILL)* Where is he?

BILL. In the next room. I'll call him in. *(Going to door.)* Mr. Bell?

(MR. BELL strides into the room angrily.)

BILL. Mr. North, this is Mr. Bell. Mr. Bell, this is Mr. North.

(THEOPHILUS holds out his hand. MR. BELL ignores him.)

AUGUSTUS BELL. *(Out)* I do not shake hands with tennis coaches.

BILL. Mr. Bell, I suggest you let me start the story. If I get anything wrong you can correct me.

(MR. BELL grunts.)

BILL. As I told you, Mr. Bell has a daughter, Miss Diana, a most attractive young woman with a host of friends, perhaps a little restless and self-willed. Can I say that, Mr. Bell?

(MR. BELL grumbles.)

BILL. It has been discovered that Miss Diana is planning to elope, as she has once before, when police were alerted in four states and she was brought home. The scandal papers went wild with it.

AUGUSTUS BELL. Bill! Get on with it!

BILL. Well apparently it's happening again. Mrs. Bell has come across a letter hidden in her daughter's lingerie, from a man, containing plans for a trip to Maryland where they intend on getting married day after tomorrow.

AUGUSTUS BELL. The hell they are!

THEOPHILUS. Who is the man?

BILL. Hilary Jones is the head of the athletics staffs in the schools system, and a substitute science teacher. He's thirty-two, divorced, and has a small ailing daughter. He is well-thought-of by everybody.

AUGUSTUS BELL. Oh God, Bill! He's a nobody. A God-damned fortune-hunter. He's trash.

THEOPHILUS. Whose car are they driving?

BILL. On the ten p.m. ferry to Saunderstown they will be in his car, the school athletics truck.

AUGUSTUS BELL. Stop! I can't stand it!

BILL. Mr. Bell, it is important that Mr. North know the facts if he's—

AUGUSTUS BELL. The only fact he needs to know is that Hilary Jones is a vulgar, unscrupulous, gold-digging bastard. It's obvious.

THEOPHILUS. Do you have Mr. Jones' letter with you, Mr. Bell?

AUGUSTUS BELL. Yes, here it is, and to hell with it!

(He throws a letter onto the floor in front of THEOPHILUS.)

BILL. Mr. Bell, we are asking Mr. North to help us.

AUGUSTUS BELL. *(Seething)* I am in a disturbed state. I apologize for throwing the letter on the floor.

BILL. Mr. and Mrs. Bell hope you will be successful, for which they will "thank you" most generously.

AUGUSTUS BELL. I'm ready to pay you five-hundred dollars.

BILL. I thought you said a thousand.

AUGUSTUS BELL. Jesus Christ, Bill!

THEOPHILUS. That is generous, indeed. And for so magnanimous a show of gratitude, what are your expectations, Mr. Bell? What's your idea I would do?

AUGUSTUS BELL. Follow them. Wait till they stop for the night. Put their car out of order. Beat down their door. Tell her what an idiot she is, and then bring her back.

THEOPHILUS. In that case, Mr. Bell, you must hire someone to kidnap your daughter. No amount of money could hire me to do that.

BILL. All Mr. Bell is asking you, as a favor from one Yale man to another, is to try.

THEOPHILUS. All right, I'll do it. But understand that mine is only a mission of persuasion. I will send you a bill for the exact amount I lose for canceling my engagements here. That's compensation for time, not payment for guaranteed success, since I am doing this as a favor for Bill. And I want a car placed at my disposal. But, most important, whether I succeed or fail, I promise I shall say nothing about this matter to anyone outside your family. Agreed?

(Pause, as he holds his hand out to MR. BELL, who grudgingly shakes it.)

AUGUSTUS BELL. Agreed.
THEOPHILUS. I'll return tonight to pick up the car.

(Scene shifts into the ferry.)

THEOPHILUS. *(Out)* And the car I get is a beauty! The first I see of the couple is as their car boards the ferry.

WOMAN 3. *(Appearing)* I am the ferry boat between Newport and Saunderstown. I represent the seaport section of the city, redolent of tar and oakum, drying nets and damp wooden docks. Eight autos in the hull is a full load. Crossing takes about one hour and a quarter, unless there's a headwind—then it's a little more. But tonight there's no headwind, so no need to worry.

(She goes.)

THEOPHILUS. *(Out, as DIANA and HILARY enter.)* I follow them into the dimly lit hull. She sees me, too.

DIANA. I know who you are. You work at the Casino. You have been paid by my father to spy on me. You are beneath contempt! You are the lowest form of human life! I could spit on you! *(Pause)* Well?

THEOPHILUS. I am here in one capacity. I am here to represent common sense.

DIANA. Ha!

THEOPHILUS. This will call down a world of ridicule in the papers—

DIANA. Rubbish!

HILARY. *(To THEOPHILUS)* Now, wait a minute—

THEOPHILUS. You will ruin Mr. Jones' career as a teacher—

DIANA. Nonsense!

THEOPHILUS. I hope that you'll marry Mr. Jones—and with your family sitting in the front pew, as is fitting of a woman of your class and distinction.

DIANA. I can't stand it! Being hounded by snooping detectives and—I'm going crazy! I just want to be free to do what I want!

HILARY. Diana, let's hear what he has to say.

DIANA. Hear him? Hear him? That yellow-bellied spy?

HILARY. Diana! Listen to me!

DIANA. How dare you give orders to me!

(She slaps him.)

THEOPHILUS. *(Out)* She slapped him!

HILARY. *(Out)* Resoundingly.

DIANA. I won't be followed! I'll never go back to that house again. Why can't I live like other people?

THEOPHILUS. Miss Bell, I want to spare you and Mr. Jones a great deal of mortification in the future.

HILARY. Diana, you're not acting like the girl I met a month ago.

DIANA. But, Hilary, can't you see? He's trying to cage us in. To block us.

THEOPHILUS. This crossing will take about half an hour more. May we go to the upper deck and talk this matter over reasonably?

HILARY. Diana, please—maybe we should listen to what he has to say.

DIANA. Oh... all right, then!

WOMAN 3. *(Reappearing)* The sandwich and coffee counter:

my tables and chairs have grown stained and rusted. I am lit by a
steel-blue lamp which would cause any decent-looking person to
resemble a criminal's photograph. At this hour, the sandwiches
are gone, and there's no more coffee. But you're welcome to use
the counter.

(She goes.)

DIANA. How could you take this nasty job, Mr. North?

THEOPHILUS. I'll tell you anything you want to know
about me later. But I'd like to hear from you first.

DIANA. Why should I tell you anything?

HILARY. Diana, he wants to help us.

DIANA. Well... what do you want to know?

THEOPHILUS. How did you first meet?

DIANA. I met Hilary at the hospital where I do volunteer
work. I saw him talking with his daughter, Linda, smiling at her.
Most fathers just bring a gift and act as though they wished they
were a thousand miles away. I fell in love just watching him.

THEOPHILUS. Were you as immediately taken with Miss
Bell, Mr. Jones?

HILARY. When I first saw Diana I thought she was the most
beautiful person I'd ever seen: in a blue-striped uniform, sitting
beside a patient's bed. I didn't know she came from one of the
big families. I wanted to call on her parents, but she thought it
wouldn't do any good... that the only thing to do is what we're
doing tonight.

DIANA. I love you, Hilary, and want you to forgive me for
slapping you. Mr. North, I lose control every now and then. My
whole life has been mixed up and full of mistakes. I was sent
home from three schools. If you and my father pull me back to

Newport this time, I'll put an end to myself. I have a little money of my own, and there are schools and colleges all over Maryland where Hilary can go on with his work.

THEOPHILUS. Miss Bell, you've run out of your allowance of elopements. I hate to say it, but you have a nickname known by millions who read those Sunday tabloids.

DIANA. What?

THEOPHILUS. I'm not going to tell you.

DIANA. What is it?

THEOPHILUS. I'm not going to be part of cheap journalists' chatter.

DIANA. Well, what do you suggest, Dr. Commonsense?

THEOPHILUS. This is the last ferry of the night. When we get off, we must drive to Providence then back down to Newport. Let's take one car so we can talk, and we'll send for the other in the morning. I have some suggestions as to how you may marry Mr. Jones in simplicity and dignity.

DIANA. How.

THEOPHILUS. I have some newspaper friends in Newport. Articles will appear about the remarkable Mr. Jones. He'll be proposed for "Rhode Island's Teacher of the Year." That should at least break the ice with your father.

HILARY. I don't want my name mixed up in a scandal, Diana. Think about Linda. Don't you think it's best that we go back?

DIANA. *(To THEOPHILUS)* You devil.

(She bursts into tears.)

THEOPHILUS. *(Out)* She weeps profusely as we transfer their luggage into my car, stopping only to say—

DIANA. I don't want to sit by *that man*.

THEOPHILUS. *(Out)* So she sits by the window and falls asleep, or seems to. As we reach the periphery of Providence it is nearly midnight and it begins to rain, so it is necessary to wake Diana to close the window.

(DIANA rolls up the window, opens her handbag, takes out a pack of cigarettes and lights one. HILARY turns to stone.)

HILARY. *(Out)* She smokes.

THEOPHILUS. There's still an hour's drive. I need a little drink to keep me awake.

DIANA. Me, too.

HILARY. *(Out)* She drinks.

THEOPHILUS. You don't drink, do you, Hilary? Well, you can come along and be our bodyguard. *(Out)* I am not a drinking man either—unless the opportunity arises. We pull up to a private club open at that hour.

HILARY. *(Reading a sign)* The Polish-American Friendship Society.

THEOPHILUS. *(Out)* Very dark, well-attended, and cordial. We're not even allowed to pay for our drinks. Diana is surrounded by men.

DIANA. *(To imaginary club member.)* You're gorgeous yourself, brother. Yes, I'd love to dance with you!

(She exits.)

HILARY. *(Out)* She dances with strangers.

THEOPHILUS. I hear you are a man of science, as well as the body, Hilary.

HILARY. Only a substitute. Whenever Mr. Gilchrist gets a bad head cold or his wife is having a baby.

THEOPHILUS. I'm fascinated by the sciences.

HILARY. I stick to the basics. You know, acids, bases, catalysts—that kind of stuff.

THEOPHILUS. Catalysts! Now those intrigue me. An external agent which promotes change between other elements, yes?

HILARY. Very good, Mr. North. I'm impressed. But you know what I find most interesting about catalysts?

THEOPHILUS. Tell me.

HILARY. They never change. The other components have altered their fundamental relationship. But not the catalyst—doesn't shrink or grow, forms no permanent bonds.

THEOPHILUS. Really... then this evening has been both entertaining *and* informative.

HILARY. You have no idea...

THEOPHILUS. Hill, do you have a contract with the Board of Education?

HILARY. Yes.

THEOPHILUS. You're not breaking it, are you? *(Silence)* Does Miss Bell know that? Does she know that you couldn't get another job like your own in the whole country if you break it? That the only jobs you could get would be in athletic clubs for middle-aged men trying to lose weight?

HILARY. No.

THEOPHILUS. Have you sent in your letter of resignation yet?

HILARY. No. *(Pause)* Don't you see? We loved each other so much. It all looked so easy.

(They watch DIANA dancing, off.)

HILARY. Theophilus, I want you to help me break this up.

THEOPHILUS. The party?

HILARY. No, the whole thing.

THEOPHILUS. I think it already is, Hill. On the way home I want you to talk without stopping about your sports teams. Everything. *(To DIANA)* I guess we'd better get on the road, Miss Bell.

HILARY. It's stopped raining.

DIANA. *(Entering)* Gentlemen, I haven't had such a good time in years. My shoes are ruined—the big brutes!

THEOPHILUS. *(Out)* We drive off and get down to the subject of sports.

HILARY. Wendell Fusco at Washington's a real comer. You should see that boy lower his head and crash through the line. He's going to Brown year after next. But I'll confess to you that the most exciting event of the year is the All-Newport Relay Race. You have no idea how different the boys are from one another. Take Bylinsky, he's the captain of the blue team. He's not as fast as some of the others, but he's the thinker. Imagine this: he likes to run second. *(THEOPHILUS' next lines overlap.)* He knows the good points and the bad points of each of his team and every inch of the course...

THEOPHILUS. *(Out)* I don't need to imagine. I feel like I'm listening to Homer.

HILARY. Then fair-haired Thetis raised her eyes to Zeus the thunderer and prayed for her son...

THEOPHILUS. *(Out)* On goes the catalogue.

HILARY. Then there's Bobby Neuthaler. Kind of excitable. Bursts into tears at the end of every race, win or lose... *(Overlap.)* The other guys respect it, though, pretend not to see it...

THEOPHILUS. *(Out)* I glance at Diana, neglected, forgotten.

HILARY. ...even for Achilles, whom she bore to Peleus, King of the Myrmidons.

THEOPHILUS. *(Out)* Her eyes are open, lost in deep thought.

HILARY. ...Golly, I wish you could see Roger Ciccolino pick up that stick; just a little runt, but puts his whole soul into it...

THEOPHILUS. *(Out)* We arrive at the door of Hilary's rooming house well after one and take his suitcase from the car. Diana looks about the deserted street of a Newport area where she has seldom put down her foot.

(MAN 1 appears.)

MAN 1. The Middle Class town: as I always am, always have been, and long will be. My inhabitants go about their lives in a timeless way. Sweeping their steps, calling to their neighbors, listening to their church bells. Buying their sundries and paying their bills. Raising their children and burying their dead.

(He goes.)

DIANA. Hilary, I slapped your face. Will you please slap mine so we'll be quits, fair and even?

HILARY. No, Diana!

DIANA. Please.

HILARY. No. I thank you for the many happy weeks we had. And your kindness to Linda. Will you give me a kiss for her?

(She kisses his cheek and gets in the car. HILARY goes. They

drive in silence for a good while.)

THEOPHILUS. Do you like music, Miss Bell?

DIANA. What? Did you——? What did you say?

THEOPHILUS. Do you like music?

DIANA. No. *(Long pause.)* Jazz. I like jazz.

THEOPHILUS. Ah. *(Pause.)* What about classical, or opera?

DIANA. God help us. In the city sometimes Father makes us go with him to the opera. To be seen. German ones are the longest; they never shut up.

(Long pause, as they drive.)

THEOPHILUS. What about art?

DIANA. What? No. *(Beat.)* Except one. I once saw a painting I liked. By one of those French fellows. Of a river, lined with trees... with a boat on it. And I think there was a bridge. That one I liked. I asked my father to buy it for me for my birthday.

THEOPHILUS. Did he?

DIANA. No. He said he wouldn't pay that kind of money for a picture of a boat that was blurry.

THEOPHILUS. What did he get you instead?

DIANA. A boat.

THEOPHILUS. *(Out)* We arrive at the great gates of her home. *(To Diana.)* It seems there's some kind of party going on inside.

DIANA. Mahjongg. Everybody's mad about mahjongg. It's tournament night. Please drive around to the back door. I don't want anyone to see me.

THEOPHILUS. *(Out)* I carry her luggage to the darkened back entrance.

DIANA. Hold me a minute. *(She begins to put her arms around him.)* This is not an embrace; it doesn't count if our faces don't touch.

THEOPHILUS. *(Out)* She's right. My objectivity is secure if our faces don't touch. *(They hold each other for a moment, then he breaks it.)* You're trembling.

DIANA. Am I? I thought that was you. *(Beat.)* Strange.

THEOPHILUS. What, Miss Bell?

DIANA. I don't know you. But because of you I won't be marrying Hilary.

THEOPHILUS. Are you angry?

DIANA. Because of four hours with you, my life will be different. Strange, I think.

THEOPHILUS. *(Out)* Throughout the evening I've been lying—about my "friends" on the newspaper, about Diana's tabloid nickname... But I had a job to do for Bill. And I knew this marriage would have been disastrous—wouldn't it? *(To DIANA)* Miss Bell—

DIANA. *(Quietly)* Listen. You can hear the servants in the kitchen.

THEOPHILUS. *(Out)* She has only to ring the bell and she will be gone.

DIANA. *(Out)* And I do.

(DIANA goes.)

THEOPHILUS. Miss Bell— *(She is not there.)* Four hours and a life is changed. By me. I changed a life. *(Lights come up on the Bell's tableau.)* Miss Bell? I... I didn't know. Come back and I'll... I'll... It was adventure! It was supposed to be fun!

(Into:)

Scene 5
At Mrs. Cranston's, iii

THEOPHILUS. Simple adventure and fun! That's all I wanted!

MRS. CRANSTON. Are you not finding that here, Theophilus?

THEOPHILUS. Well, yes... and more!

MRS. CRANSTON. And what is that?

THEOPHILUS. Complications! Confusion! Maybe I'm just having the wrong kinds of adventure. It will be different in Europe. They're very advanced there. Europe!

MRS. CRANSTON. Then why don't you go?

THEOPHILUS. Money, Mrs. Cranston. If there's one thing I've discovered while being here in Newport, it's this: the rich never pay. I doubt if what I have in my pocket would take me further than some small New Hampshire town just across the Massachusetts line.

MRS. CRANSTON. Then you must keep at it until you have what you need.

(HENRY enters.)

HENRY. Teddy! What's the news in the world of big words?

MRS. CRANSTON. Theophilus was just wondering what to do next. In order to facilitate his lateral maneuver across the ocean.

THEOPHILUS. Yes, I *must* get out of Newport and get to

Europe. I've got to find some new position—especially after an abrupt termination.

HENRY. *Terminated?*

MRS. CRANSTON. Astonishing.

THEOPHILUS. Do you recall, at the beginning of the summer, philosophy and the marathon reading of the *Bible*?

HENRY. Oh, you mean—?

MRS. CRANSTON. No names, Henry!

HENRY. Sorry, ma'am.

MRS. CRANSTON. I hear a kettle boiling, Theophilus. What happened?

THEOPHILUS. I'm not entirely certain. I felt like I was involved in some convoluted plot out of a late Elizabethan drama. The butler loathed me. And whenever I passed "the lady," her glance insinuated hateful things. I never really understood why almost every member of that household despised me.

(Beat.)

HENRY. Gracious lady, should we tell Teddie our theory of the Death Watch?

MRS. CRANSTON. Yes, Henry, I believe we should. I know it will interest him.

HENRY. Will you interrupt me, ma'am, if I get to sliding on the ice?

MRS. CRANSTON. Of course, Henry.

HENRY. Well, it's this way. In a dozen houses in Newport there's an aged party sitting on a mountain of money.

MRS. CRANSTON. Twenty houses, Henry, at *least* twenty.

HENRY. Yes, ma'am. Now let's call the aged party the Old Moggle.

MRS. CRANSTON. Mogul, Henry. But you can pronounce it either way. Newport's the only place in the country where rich old men live longer than rich old women. It's the social life that kills.

HENRY. Now the Death Watch has a lot to worry about. In some houses the Old Moggle has sons and daughters and grandchildren, all waiting for the reading of the will. But the Old Party won't die. So what do you do? You remind him of his health—tenderly, sadly.

MRS. CRANSTON. You call in doctors.

HENRY. Specialists.

MRS. CRANSTON. Specialists! Specialists are the Death Watchers' best friend.

HENRY. All men over seventy can be made into high-pepper-condriacs in zero time with a little attention from the loved ones.

MRS. CRANSTON. In other houses anyone the Old Mogul takes a liking to, any new favorite, is a threat.

HENRY. And the Death Watch begins to panic. Expel him!

MRS. CRANSTON. And in many their "object sublime" is guardianship. Soften him up for guardianship.

HENRY. Terrible! Why, we know a Moggle who hasn't left his front door for ten years.

MRS. CRANSTON. Seven, Henry.

HENRY. You never know when Teddie might come up against an example of things like this.

MRS. CRANSTON. No, Henry, you never know. Theophilus, if you can't find adventure under that roof now, I don't know where you ever will. But I'll say no more.

(MRS. CRANSTON and HENRY go. DR. BOSWORTH appears.)

Scene 6
Nine Gables, iii

THEOPHILUS. Good morning.

DR. BOSWORTH. Theophilus, my dear boy! But where have you been?!

THEOPHILUS. I was detained, and for that I apologize. But I am back now. Dr. Bosworth, I think it would be a great privilege to visit Berkeley's Whitehall in your company. Would it be possible to drive out some afternoon and see the house together?

DR. BOSWORTH. Indeed, I wish we could. I thought you understood: I am unable to leave this house for more than a quarter of an hour. I shall die here. You know, Theophilus, it had always been my dream to buy Whitehall and fifty surrounding acres, then build an Academy of Philosophers there. It was a great secret. I wanted to invite the leading philosophers of the world.

THEOPHILUS. To come and lecture here?

DR. BOSWORTH. No, to come and live here! Each would have been given his own house. Alfred Whitehead, Bertrand Russell, Wittgenstein! If he isn't dead... Newport would have become like a great lighthouse of elevated thought. But there was so much planning to be done, and...

THEOPHILUS. And what...?

DR. BOSWORTH. Theophilus, I suffer from a disorder of the kidneys which may be related to a fatal disease. I find this very strange because I have experienced no pain. I suffer from a compulsion to urinate—or try to urinate—every ten to fifteen minutes.

THEOPHILUS. But, Dr. Bosworth, you and I have sat in

your study for hours at a time without your ever leaving the room.

DR. BOSWORTH. Isn't that the ridiculous part? As long as I'm in my own house, keeping quiet, I am not inconvenienced. I am told it's not the usual old man's affliction. It's something far graver.

THEOPHILUS. Who told you this?

DR. BOSWORTH. Specialists. Medical men my daughter has brought in. I must rely on their word.

THEOPHILUS. I see.

DR. BOSWORTH. Mr. North, it *breaks* me to think I'm trapped here. What experiences I've had. My vision has autographed the air of such places. The worst of it is the idea is getting around that I'm crazy. Perhaps I am. Do you think I'm crazy?

THEOPHILUS. No, Dr. Bosworth, I don't. And this kidney trouble—I know all about it. I drove a truck one summer in Florida, and it was hell on the kidneys. I know a place in town that sells a special pill and a certain "gadget." It's got a very vulgar name that I won't repeat to you. I'm going to get it for you and then we'll try it out on a drive to Whitehall.

DR. BOSWORTH. *(Almost weeping)* If you do that, Mr. North, if you do that, I'll believe there's a God. I will. Nietzsche be damned!

SARAH. *(Entering)* Father, who are you talking— *Mr. North!* I thought it was understood that— that you— *How* did you get in here?

THEOPHILUS. There are more ways to enter a structure than through a door. Read Feydeau.

SARAH. Father, say goodbye to Mr. North. The doctor is convinced that these extended hours are harmful to you.

DR. BOSWORTH. My compliments to the doctor. *(To THEOPHILUS)* Let me see you out, Mr. North. I'll expect you Tuesday evening. *(Quietly)* Perhaps I shall live again.

(SARAH exits.)

THEOPHILUS. *(Out)* And to think I almost didn't go back to him; turned my back upon a tethered kindred spirit. I go to the store which I mentioned. I purchase some mild aspirin, and one of those... gadgets. I buy a size "medium" and call the good Doctor.

DR. BOSWORTH. *(Entering)* Hello? Mr. North? Hello?

THEOPHILUS. I have a message for you. Can I give it to you on this line?

DR. BOSWORTH. Yes. I've snuck into the gardener's shed.

THEOPHILUS. In a quarter of an hour a parcel is going to arrive for your hands only. Don't let anyone intercept it. When you take your walk around the garden this afternoon, take one of the pills. Thousands of men take them on the road every day. The other thing is just a safeguard. You'll be able to throw it away after a week or two.

DR. BOSWORTH. I don't know what to say. I'll be at the front door in a quarter of an hour, and report to you Tuesday night.

Scene 7
Myra, v

THEOPHILUS. *(Out)* On the way to my next appointment with Myra, I pass Fort Adams, where my brother served in the Navy, defending Narragansett Bay.

(MAN 2 appears.)

MAN 2. I am a city unto myself, that of the Army and Navy in Newport. With high-fenced borders surrounding acres of barracks, I am a world apart. Identical dwellings, identical streets, identical conventions. Hundreds of Penelopes within are anticipating the return of their own Ulysses, awaiting the reappearance of the face with which they first fell in love.

(He goes.)

THEOPHILUS. *(Out)* I enter Myra's afternoon room. Neither she nor Mrs. Cummings is present. However, there is a young man of about twenty-four.

YOUNG MAN. *(It is MYRA, dressed as a man.)* Mr. North, I believe. I am Ceasar Nielson, Myra Granberry's twin brother.

THEOPHILUS. Is your sister at home, Mr. Nielson?

MYRA. I thought perhaps one day soon it would be nice to drive out and ask your friend Mademoiselle Desmoulins to join us for a drink.

THEOPHILUS. Sir, I am employed here to read English literature with Mrs. Granberry. She appears to be late for our appointment. Will you be joining us?

MYRA. My twin sister Myra tells me that badgers fight to defend what they've got.

THEOPHILUS. Yes, but since nature made them small, she also made them clever. As a rule, Mr. Nielson, no well-conditioned badger destroys its home to preserve it.

MRS. CUMMINGS. *(Entering)* He's on his way up, Mrs. Granberry.

MYRA. Cora, you've ruined my disguise for Mr. North!

THEOPHILUS. Don't worry, Mrs. Cummings, I had begun to suspect it on my own.

MYRA. Theophilus, I've asked George to join us. We're going to do the trial scene from *The Merchant of Venice* and I'm going to make him play Shylock. You be Antonio, I'll be Portia, and Cora will be everybody else. Cora, I want you to be splendid as the Duke. *(There is a knock at the door. GEORGE enters.)* George, darling, we want you to help us—

GORGE. *(Seeing her outfit)* Myra!

MYRA. Please don't say no because it would make me very unhappy.

GEORGE. What in the—

MYRA. George, you must read Shylock. Go slowly and be very bloodthirsty. Sharpen the knife on your shoe. Mr. North is going to lean backward over the desk with his chest exposed and his hands tied behind him.

GEORGE. Now, Myra, that's enough!

MYRA. Oh, George! It's just a game! You'll get the hang of it. *Go slowly.*

GEORGE. North, I'd like to cut out your gizzard.

THEOPHILUS. You engaged me to interest your wife in reading and especially in Shakespeare. I've done that and I'm ready to resign when you pay the three bills I've sent you.

MYRA. All right, let's begin.

THEOPHILUS. You'll need your book, Myra.

MYRA. No, I won't.

MRS. CUMMINGS. Oh, Mrs. Granberry! You've memorized!

      PORTIA.

Do you confess the bond?

      ANTONIO.

I do.

      PORTIA.

Then must the Jew be merciful.

      SHYLOCK.

On what compulsion must I? Tell me that!

      PORTIA. *(Gravely, earnestly, maturely)*

The quality of mercy is not strained,

It droppeth as the gentle rain from Heaven

Upon the place beneath. It is twice blest:

It blesseth him that gives and him that takes.

It is enthroned in the hearts of kings,

It is an attribute of God himself;

And earthly power doth then show likest God's

When mercy seasons justice. Therefore, Jew,

Though justice be thy plea, consider this,

That in the course of justice, none of us

Should see salvation. We do pray for mercy;

And that same prayer doth teach us all to render

The deeds of mercy.

GEORGE. *(Throwing down the knife.)* Stop it! Just look at you!

MRS. CUMMINGS. Mrs. Granberry, play acting is a little too exciting. You always stand up and move about the room. I don't think the doctor would like that.

GEORGE. Yes, Mrs. Cummings, and I hold you responsible! You have allowed Mrs. Granberry to be influenced by... unsavory literature.

MRS. CUMMINGS. No! I assure you, Sir—if any fictional character behaved unsuitably, Mr. North would escort them back to the library at once!

GEORGE. Mrs. Cummings, you are leaving the house as soon as you can pack.

MYRA. George!

GEORGE. Pants!

MYRA. I'm an emancipated woman... like Miss Desmoulins!

GEORGE. Mr. North, will you follow me into the library?

(GEORGE and THEOPHILUS move to another space.)

THEOPHILUS. If you dismiss Mrs. Cummings as incompetent, I shall write a letter to her agency telling them what I found here.

GEORGE. You broke your promise. You told my wife about Miss Desmoulins.

THEOPHILUS. Your wife told *me* about Miss Desmoulins. She received two anonymous letters.

GEORGE. You should have told me that.

THEOPHILUS. I was engaged to be a reader, not a confidential friend of the family.

GEORGE. You're the biggest nuisance in town. Everybody's talking about you. God, I hate Yale men!

THEOPHILUS. In a difficult time Mrs. Cummings has been

your wife's *only* friend and support!

GEORGE. Well, what do you suggest I do? I can't live like a monk for half a year again just because my wife is under a doctor's care. I know a pack of men who have someone like Denise. What did I do wrong? What the hell will I do here? *Play Shakespeare all day?* Well say something! Don't just stand there like an ox! Jesus! You think I neglect Myra. I do. And I know I do. Do you know why? I... I... How old are you?

THEOPHILUS. Thirty.

GEORGE. Ever been married?

THEOPHILUS. No.

GEORGE. I... can't stand being loved. Loved? Worshipped. Overestimation freezes me. My mother overestimated me and I haven't said a sincere word to her since I was fifteen. And now Myra! I can't stand it. I can't stand the responsibility. When I come into her presence I freeze. Can you understand that?

THEOPHILUS. Can I ask you a question?

GEORGE. Go ahead. I'm numb anyway.

THEOPHILUS. What do you do in the laboratory all day?

(Pause.)

GEORGE. I hide myself. And wait for something. For things to get worse or to get better. I play war games. I play with my tin soldiers or my electric trains. If you've ever kept a secret before, please keep that.

THEOPHILUS. Do you love her?

GEORGE. Of course I do.

THEOPHILUS. Then as an inventor, Mr. Granberry, I would create some way of letting her know... before she is convinced otherwise.

GEORGE. But I never said I was a *good* inventor. What am I going to do?

THEOPHILUS. *(Handing him a book.)* How about act five, scene one?

(Lights come back up on MYRA and MRS. CUMMINGS. THEOPHILUS and GEORGE enter.)

GEORGE.
Portia, forgive me this enforced wrong,
And in the hearing of these my many friends
I swear to thee, even by thine own fair eyes
Wherein I see myself, pardon this fault
And by my soul I swear I never more
Will break an oath with thee.

MRS. CUMMINGS. *(Out)* We women love to forgive you men when you ask us to.

MYRA. *(Out)* But we won't do it forever.

GEORGE. Oh, and Myra?

MYRA. Yes, George?

GEORGE. May I have the pleasure of your company at dinner on Wednesday night at the Muenchinger-King?

MYRA. Oh, George...

(GEORGE and MYRA kiss, gently—their tableau.)

MRS. CUMMINGS. *(Out)* Learn to accept love. It's all overestimation. Accept love—with a smile, with a grin.

(The GRANBERRYS and MRS. CUMMINGS go.)

Scene 8
Nine Gables, iv

DR. BOSWORTH. *(Entering and clutching THEOPHILUS)* First afternoon, half an hour! This morning, half an hour! This afternoon, forty-five minutes!

THEOPHILUS. That's wonderful!

DR. BOSWORTH. It's miraculous! Mr. North, can you drive with me to Whitehall this Sunday?

THEOPHILUS. It would be a great privilege.

DR. BOSWORTH. Mr. North, you've never driven a truck in your life, have you?

THEOPHILUS. Certainly I have. One summer in— Well, not for more than two miles, no... And it was a school bus... Which then required a new transmission.

DR. BOSWORTH. Then how on earth did you know about *this*?

THEOPHILUS. One can learn a lot from an older brother in the Army.

(SARAH BOSWORTH enters.)

SARAH. Father, send Mr. North home. We simply cannot have any more of this strange and agitated behavior.

DR. BOSWORTH. Sarah, tomorrow I want you to arrange for a car and chauffeur for my use. I wish to go for a drive at four-thirty, after my nap.

SARAH. You are not going to—?!

DR. BOSWORTH. What you take for my strange behavior is an improvement in my health.

SARAH. A drive! Without the doctor's permission!

DR. BOSWORTH. I do not now feel the need of a doctor. I wish to return to my studies.

SARAH. But we are all deeply concerned. We love you!

DR. BOSWORTH. Then you'll be glad to hear that I feel much better. This Sunday Mr. North and I are going to Whitehall. I'll meet you in the study momentarily, Mr. North. I want your opinion on some plans for the Academy.

(He exits. THEOPHILUS begins to exit towards the study.)

SARAH. Stay here, young man. There has been a fearsome storm gathering about your head for some time.

THEOPHILUS. I enjoy flashes of lightning, Mrs. Bosworth.

SARAH. The time has come for stronger measures. Since you entered this house you have been a constant source of confusion. I regard you as a foolish and dangerous boy. Will you explain to me what you are trying to do to my father?

THEOPHILUS. I don't understand what you mean, Mrs. Bosworth.

SARAH. These exertions may kill him.

THEOPHILUS. Your father invited me to accompany him to Whitehall. I assumed he was capable of determining for himself how he felt.

SARAH. Assumed. It is not your business to assume anything. You are a trouble-maker. You are a vulgar intruder and you are to leave this house *immediately.*

THEOPHILUS. Excuse me. I am expected in the study.

SARAH. I forbid you to take one step further.

THEOPHILUS. Dr. Bosworth needs me to—

SARAH. My father does not need you for anything. None of

us needs you.

THEOPHILUS. Your father has—

SARAH. Precisely. He is *my* father. You may not have him. Get one of your own.

THEOPHILUS. I beg your pardon?

SARAH. For the last three months I have heard of your inane antics and meddling in this town. I see what you are, and it is pathetic. Vainly attempting to insinuate yourself into a family, trying to be one of us.

THEOPHILUS. I never—

SARAH. No, you never will. Don't you have people? Go back to them. Or don't they want you either?

THEOPHILUS. I have—

SARAH. You have nothing.

(Pause.)

THEOPHILUS. I have all of you.

SARAH. And what do you mean by that?

THEOPHILUS. All of you. I have a sister who is the Countess of the Aquidneck Isles at the age of fourteen. A brother who is the King of France and who can conjugate all the irregular verbs. I have a fiancée, so desperate to prove her capacity for love, that she would run across seven state lines to marry me. I have a wife who dresses as Portia to bear me a child. And I have a grandfather who reads Berkeley to me in his library from a nineteenth-century chair.

SARAH. In what narcotic fantasy do you reside, Mr. North? With which of those family members will you be dining tonight? I will be dining with my father, whom I love.

THEOPHILUS. Control and manipulation are not synonymous with love.

SARAH. Pray, teach me more about love, Professor North. Interesting lessons coming from a boy who has no connections to anyone as far as I can see. You are nowhere, with no one.

THEOPHILUS. And you, Mrs. Bosworth, are very pale. Are you unwell? *(Louder)* Can I get you a glass of water?

SARAH. Lower your voice.

THEOPHILUS. *(Running about)* Mr. Willis! Mr. Willis! Is anybody there? Help!

SARAH. Stop this nonsense. I am fine.

THEOPHILUS. Smelling salts! Call a doctor! Help!

SARAH. Be quiet!

THEOPHILUS. Unlace her! Break a window! Give us some AIR!

SARAH. *(With great clarity, getting his attention)* Mr. North! *(Pause, as she sees through him, almost tenderly)* Who loves *you*, Mr. North? To whom do you *offer* love?

(THEOPHILUS slowly sinks into a chair. DR. BOSWORTH and WILLIS enter.)

DR. BOSWORTH. What's the matter, Sarah?

SARAH. Nothing. The boy was not well. He has come to his senses now.

DR. BOSWORTH. Willis, Mr. North and I will have whisky and soda.

SARAH. Whisky? Surely the doctor would advise against that, Father.

DR. BOSWORTH. I hear a little whisky in the evening has medicinal value. And Mr. North looks like he could use it.

SARAH. All right, Father. I will go check on our dinner.

(SARAH and WILLIS exit.)

DR. BOSWORTH. Are you unwell, Mr. North?

THEOPHILUS. No, Dr. Bosworth, thank you. But I shall have to discontinue my visits.

DR. BOSWORTH. What? But, Mr. North, the Academy! Stay and be part of the lighthouse of elevated thought: rising high above the ordinary, the commonplace, the pedestrian.

THEOPHILUS. Dr. Bosworth, two months ago, a week ago, perhaps even minutes ago, nothing would have been more appealing to me. But at this moment... No, Dr. Bosworth, I must go.

DR. BOSWORTH. Yes. Yes, of course you must. We know about these things, don't we?

THEOPHILUS. And you? You're a man of freedom again, Dr. Bosworth. Where will you go?

DR. BOSWORTH. I believe I'll enjoy the Ten-Mile Drive of Newport daily. Perhaps go to New York in the Fall. But there is someplace I wish greatly to go first.

THEOPHILUS. Where is that?

DR. BOSWORTH. In to dinner with my daughter, Mr. North. *(He begins to exit, then—)* By the way, Theophilus, as I said before, that Getting-Up-and-Leaving-the-Room trick is very effective. I did it all the time. But I began to wonder if... Well, often the next room is... just another room.

(SARAH and DR. BOSWORTH come together in a Nine Gables tableau, then are gone.)

Scene 9
The Constellations

(MRS. CRANSTON and HENRY appear.)

HENRY. Get a move on, Teddy! Tonight is the Servants' Ball, to celebrate the closing of the summer season!

MRS. CRANSTON. Henry Simmons, you know that only servants are allowed.

HENRY. Now, Mrs. Cranston, we could tell a little lie just this once and say he was a servant.

MRS. CRANSTON. No, Henry. Theophilus knows the first rule: there are those who go in the front door and those who don't.

HENRY. It's difficult to believe the season has passed.

MRS. CRANSTON. Yes, it can be like cold water to realize how quickly things change. Theophilus, at our first meeting I surmised that by now you would have made your observations about Newport. I am most eager to hear you thoughts, if you are willing to share them.

THEOPHILUS. Mrs. Cranston, I've discovered that persons endowed with enormous inherited wealth are not so different really. They feel the need to belong, so they herd together for company, and take comfort in the warming satisfaction of exclusion. Fear can do that: close others out and reject in the name of safety and solace.

MRS. CRANSTON. Oh, Theophilus, you *do* have the muse.

THEOPHILUS. *(Pause)* I— what I'm about to say... I find it difficult.

MRS. CRANSTON. It needn't be.

HENRY. *(To MRS. CRANSTON)* I suppose I'd best tell him now.

MRS. CRANSTON. All right, Henry.

HENRY. *(Quietly)* She said yes, cully.

THEOPHILUS. Who said yes?

HENRY. Edweena.

MRS. CRANSTON. Before she went on her trip, Mr. Simmons asked her to be his wife. She said she would let him know.

THEOPHILUS. I thought she was in the Bahamas.

HENRY. She is, cully. Look: she sent me a telegram saying "yes." Her love sent to me under the ocean through a tiny wire—and I felt it.

(Beat)

MRS. CRANSTON. Theophilus?

THEOPHILUS. Congratulations, Henry. That's wonderful news. Wonderful.

HENRY. Cheers, Teddie.

MRS. CRANSTON. At midnight, Theophilus, ride past under the windows of the main hall. I will have the band play the "Blue Danube Waltz." Mr. Simmons and I will be dancing, and thinking of you.

(MRS. CRANSTON and HENRY go. JOSIAH DEXTER appears.)

JOSIAH. Hello again, Mr. North. You want to say a few words to Hannah?

THEOPHILUS. No, Mr. Dexter. I'm not so light-headed as I was. But if she's fixed, I'd like to buy her back from you.

JOSIAH. When would you like to pick her up?

THEOPHILUS. If you give me the key, I can return the bicycle tomorrow morning and take her without disturbing you.

JOSIAH. Mr. North, I have a confession to make. A few weeks ago my brother gave me a story; said he cleaned it out of one of the old cars. The adventure a young man has with a shoemaker's daughter in Trenton. No name on it. I now think that story was by you. *(He hands a story to THEOPHILUS.)* Will you accept my apology, Mr. North?

THEOPHILUS. Just some scribbling to pass the time.

JOSIAH. You made it pretty vivid, Mr. North. I'd say you have a knack for that kind of thing. Ever thought of being a writer?

(Pause.)

THEOPHILUS. Please put a big can of gasoline in the car.

JOSIAH. Drive carefully, Theophilus.

(He goes. THEOPHILUS mounts his bicycle and peddles, slowly.)

THEOPHILUS. *(Out)* It is dusk. I ride along the ocean, on the other side of which much of Portugal is sound asleep. I can almost feel the great globe rotating beneath my wheels as I ride by the amazing homes of each person I have met. When I get to the Fenwick's, strolling barefoot on the lawn by the front gate...

(ELOISE appears.)

ELOISE. Hello, Mr. North.

THEOPHILUS. Hello, Eloise. How is your family?

ELOISE. They are fine, thank you. Charles is on a camping

trip with some friends.

THEOPHILUS. Wonderful. Shouldn't you be having supper? What are you doing out here?

ELOISE. You might laugh.

THEOPHILUS. Never.

ELOISE. Each evening I say goodnight to the flowers, and hello to the stars.

THEOPHILUS. Eloise, you are a child of Heaven.

ELOISE. Why did you say that?

THEOPHILUS. It just sprang to my lips. *(Pause)* Is Charles still planning a trip to Paris?

ELOISE. Absolument, Monsieur le professeur.

THEOPHILUS. And what about you? Do you have any plans?

ELOISE. Yes. But you must promise not to say one word about it to anyone.

THEOPHILUS. I promise.

ELOISE. I want to be a nun. I'm so grateful to God for my family, for the sun and the sea, that I want to give my life to Him.

THEOPHILUS. But, Eloise—

ELOISE. I'm learning to pray. I want to love everybody on earth as much as I love my family. I want to love God above all. What do *you* want, Mr. North?

THEOPHILUS. I don't know. Throughout the summer I've been lying. To myself. I want...

ELOISE. What?

THEOPHILUS. I don't know.

ELOISE. *(Pointing to the stars)* Look! It's the dragon!

THEOPHILUS. Draco, guardian of treasures.

(They sit together on the grass.)

ELOISE. Papa says *that* one is made up of eighteen stars. That half the year he appears upside down, but during the summer, as the universe moves, he raises his head upright. And there's the North Star.

THEOPHILUS. Where?

ELOISE. Over there, by itself.

THEOPHILUS. Not by itself, Eloise. Surrounded by them all. *(They sit silently, gazing at the stars, then—)* Eloise... That is what I want. I want to be surrounded... By... a Constellation. Of people. Made up of eighteen stars. I... I want to have nine male friends—

(The MEN and WOMEN are revealed.)

MAN 3. three older than yourself,

MAN 1. three younger,

MAN 2. and three of your own age.

THEOPHILUS. And I want to have nine female friends—

WOMAN 3. three older,

ELOISE. younger,

WOMAN 2. and of the same age.

THEOPHILUS. It is likely that seldom,

MAN 2. perhaps never,

WOMAN 3. will all eighteen spots be filled at the same time.

MAN 1. Vacancies will occur.

WOMAN 2. Some stars will be short-lived,

MAN 3. Some you may never have,

MAN 2. And some will last a lifetime.

THEOPHILUS. And I want to know that my star plays a part in the Constellations of others. Then, what a deep satisfaction I will feel when each vacant place is filled. Like a watcher of the skies when a new planet swims into my ken.

    ELOISE. Oh, Mr. North...

    THEOPHILUS. Eloise, say a prayer for me sometimes, too?

    ELOISE. Wherever you are in the world, I shall be praying for you. Goodbye, Mr. North.

(ELOISE goes, joining the Constellation as WOMAN 1. There is a long pause as the Constellation, around him, watches.)

    WOMAN 3. It was the spring and summer of 1926.

    THEOPHILUS. Slowly and wonderingly one raises one's head.

    MAN 3. Memory and The Imagination combined can do miraculous things.

    THEOPHILUS. They can even make a writer, if that's what they want to do.

(The following six lines overlap somewhat, until WOMAN 2's final line, said alone.)

    WOMAN 2. "As I rode, I gazed across the glittering see towards Portugal..."

    WOMAN 3. "Mrs. Cranston's was a large establishment built in the shadow of Trinity Church..."

    MAN 3. "Sea Ledges derived its name from its vast lawns and gardens which gently sloped..."

    WOMAN 1. "Eloise, eyes sparkling, cupped her hand to my ear and shared, 'I am a part of all that I have seen...'"

    MAN 2. "At the back door, in the darkness of the sandstone carriage gate, Diana whispered, 'Because of four hours with you, my life will be different...'"

MAN 1. "Mrs. Cummings glanced quickly at George and Myra, then back to me before I left the room. She smiled warmly, and softly said,"

WOMAN 2. "'Accept... love.'"

THEOPHILUS. I do not want to live in a lighthouse, firmly constructed so that nothing gets in. There must be no lonelier existence in the world. And I do not need to be in Hong Kong,

WOMAN 2. or Rome,

MAN 1. or Berlin,

MAN 2. or London,

WOMAN 1. or even New York

THEOPHILUS. to belong to the world. I will belong to it wherever I am.

(Theophilus's FATHER and MOTHER appear.)

FATHER. *(Gently)* Theophilus?
MOTHER. *(Quietly)* Where are you?
THEOPHILUS. Here. I'm right here.

(Lights dim on the MEN and WOMEN as they watch THEOPHILUS. THEOPHILUS views the skies.)

(Curtain.)

TRANSLATIONS OF SCENES IN FRENCH

Following are translations of the scenes in French between Theophilus and Charles Fenwick. With Scene 14, please keep in mind that the scene conducted entirely in French is wonderfully effective, whether the audience comprehends what is being said or not. (It is Charles' obvious blossoming which is of import; the words themselves are secondary.) Nonetheless, for those in nonprofessional productions who are not as proficient with the language, a partial translation of Scene 14 may be used—in keeping with the device used in Scene 11. If that is done, then the lines which are *italicized* in Scene 14 below should remain spoken in French.

Scene 9

Derriere: behind
Coucher: to lay down/sleep/go to bed
Pissoirs: urinals

Scene 11

THEOPHILUS. *(To CHARLES)* Good day, Charles.
CHARLES. Good day, Professor.
THEOPHILUS. Charles, you've been in Paris. After dark you must have seen certain women addressing gentlemen in a low voice from doorways and alleys. What do they usually say?

(Out) The scarlet flag is high on the mast. I can wait.

CHARLES. Will you sleep with me?

THEOPHILUS. Good! Charles, you're sitting alone at a bar and one of these young ladies slides up beside you. "Will you offer me a glass of champagne?" How do you answer, Charles? I'm waiting...

CHARLES. No, mademoiselle... thank you.... Not this evening.

THEOPHILUS. Very good, Charles! Could you make it a little more easy and charming? In France there is universal respect for women of every age and at every level of society, even when she's a prostitute. I have an idea. I'm going to pretend I'm one of those girls. You are strolling behind the Paris Opera. I think this will be good! *(Out)* I hope this doesn't damage him. *(Charles stands petrified.)* Come on, Charles. It's a play, not a cage of tigers. Good evening, my darling.

CHARLES. Good evening, mademoiselle.

THEOPHILUS. You are alone? Want a little amusement?

CHARLES. I'm busy tonight... Thank you. Perhaps another time. You are charming.

THEOPHILUS. Ooo! But, darling, I have a lovely room!

CHARLES. How do I get out of this?

THEOPHILUS. I suggest you make your departure quick, but cordial.

CHARLES. Mademoiselle, I'm late. I must run. But goodbye. *(He pats THEOPHILUS' elbow.)* Good luck, dear friend.

THEOPHILUS. Magnificent, Charles! Magnificent!

Scene 14

*(CHARLES enters, hands imaginary cape and top hat to THEO-
PHILUS.)*

CHARLES. (*With some arrogance*) *Good evening, Monsieur
Véfour.*

THEOPHILUS. Charles, just a moment. The French have a
word for cold, condescending self-importance: *morgue* (pride,
haughtiness). You would be horrified if you thought your subjects attributed that quality to you.

CHARLES. Of course! Let's start over. *Monsieur le professeur...* can we ask Eloise to see it? She's sitting right over
there.

THEOPHILUS. Yes, indeed! Let's invite her. *(Calling off.)*
Eloise, we're doing a little one-act play. Would you like to be our
audience?

ELOISE. *(Entering) But of course, monsieur le professeur!*

THEOPHILUS. Give it the works, Charles!

*(CHARLES enters, smiling. Hands imaginary cape and top hat to
THEOPHILUS, as coat-check girl.)*

CHARLES. *Good evening, mademoiselle. All goes well?*

THEOPHILUS. *(Curtsying) Good evening, Sir.* Your Grace
does us a very great honor.

CHARLES. *Ah, Henri-Paul, how are you?*

THEOPHILUS. *(As Véfour) Very well, Sir, thank you.*

CHARLES. And your wife, *how is she?*

THEOPHILUS. *Very well, Sir, she thanks you.*

CHARLES. *And the dear children?*

THEOPHILUS. *Very well, Your Grace, thank you.*

CHARLES. *Yours!* This is your son? *What is your name, sir? Frederic? Like your grandfather.* My grandfather was very fond of your grandfather. *Listen, Henri-Paul,* I need places for three people. Will this be a problem?

THEOPHILUS. *Not at all, Sir.* If Your Highness will be kind enough to follow me.

CHARLES. *Henri-Paul, it is so good to return to this place/ be back here.* Did you know, my friend, that my mother brought me here for the first time when I was twelve?

THEOPHILUS. *Truly?*

CHARLES. *Absolutely! We ate here every Sunday for years (a long time). Oh-la-la my mother!* It's true that you created a dessert named after her?

THEOPHILUS. *Yes, it is.*

CHARLES. I hope it contains a lot of sugar and cream! *But I am late and my guests are waiting for me. (To ELOISE.) My God! Can it be (This is true)? Is it possible? Ah, Madame la Marquise... dear cousin!*

ELOISE. *(Deep curtsy) My Prince! (He raises her up and kisses her hand.)*

CHARLES. *My friends, the streets are so crowded! It's the end of the world!* Sometimes we feel empty, but here the menu is always full. *Our banquet awaits!*

PROPERTIES AND COSTUMES

Following are properties and costume lists. They represent how
the New York production chose to meet the physical demands of
the play in these areas, in keeping with its own design concepts.
They are included here as a (hopefully) helpful reference, and are
not intended to imply that they are the "correct" choices. Each
production must decide for itself what costume and property
items best suit its needs.

PROPERTIES

ACT I

Scene 1
2 wooden chairs
1 wooden bench

Scene 2
2 megaphones (Man 1, Woman 3)
Towel, gum (Man 2)
Shovel (Man 1)
2 green umbrellas (Man 2, Woman 3)

Scene 4
Pool cue (Man 3)
Business card (Henry)

Scene 6
Feather duster (Woman 2)

Scene 7
Fenwick note (Theophilus)

Scene 8
Book (*Daisy Miller*, Theophilus)
Bosworth message (Theophilus)

Scene 9
Large book (*Notable Families*, Theophilus)

Scene 10
Stack of books (Woman 1)
Cane (Dr. Bosworth)
Small book (*Berkeley*, Dr. Bosworth)

Scene 12
Book (*The Scarlet Letter*, Myra)

Scene 13
Book (*The Analyst*, Dr. Bosworth)

Scene 14
2 anonymous letters (Myra)
Book (Shakespeare plays, Theophilus)

ACT II

Scene 4
Folded flag (Man 2)
Letter (Augustus Bell)
Baseball glove (Man 1)

Scene 7
3 books (*The Merchant of Venice,* Mrs. Cummings)

Scene 9
Telegram (Henry)
Story (Josiah)

COSTUMES

To accomplish quick character distinctions, certain items were
added to the basic costumes, as follows:

Theophilus
Brown plaid slacks, vest, and jacket; suspenders; cream dress
    shirt; brown shoes; brown argyle socks

Man 1
Base: Blue dress shirt, tan pants, suspenders, brown shoes, brown
    socks
Thames Street: Newsboy cap

Bill Wentworth: Cream suit jacket, blue tie, straw boater
Charles Fenwick: Cream sweater vest, blue bow tie
George Granberry: Brown tweed jacket and vest, glasses, maroon tie

Man 2

Base: Pale green dress shirt, gray pants, suspenders, brown shoes, gray socks
Henry: Gray jacket; white dress shirt and bowtie (for Act II, Scene 9)
Sea Ledges: Blue and white pinstripe jacket, white scarf
Willis: Black tuxedo jacket, cream dress shirt, white gloves, black bowtie
Hilary Jones: Cap
Army and Navy: Envelope cap

Man 3

Base: Brown pants, white dress shirt, suspenders, brown shoes, brown socks
Father: Gray suit jacket, glasses
Josiah Dexter: Red baseball cap
Lunatic: Glasses
Public park: Red drape/sash, walking stick
Mrs. Cranston's: Chauffer hat
Dr. Bosworth: Red bathrobe, black slippers, scarf, pinky ring, blue suit jacket (for Act II, Sc. 8)

Woman 1

Base: White linen skirt with lace trim, cream button-down t-shirt, brown slip-on flats
Lunatic: Glasses and scarf

Eloise Fenwick: White button-down sweater, tan cardigan, cream
    hat
Nine Gables: Glasses
Diana Bell: Cream cloth belt, flowered shoulder drape, red high
    heels, earrings

Woman 2
Base: White blouse with belt, cream wool skirt, brown high heels
Hannah: Arm sling, head bandage
Ten-Mile Drive: Cream scarf
Sarah Bosworth: Gold scarf, green suit jacket
Mrs. Fenwick: Cream hat with veils, beige gloves, beige cardigan
    sweater
Myra Granberry: Cream cardigan sweater, beaded necklace and
    earrings
Mrs. Cranston's: White apron
Ceasar Nielson: Brown vest, small pregnant belly, brown men's
    shoes, white plaid knickers, white cap

Woman 3
Base: White button-down blouse, tan skirt, black buckled shoes
Mother: Brown button-down sweater, oval brooch
Mrs. Cranston: Brown tweed suit jacket
Mrs. Cummings: Gray wraparound sweater
Ferryboat: Blue raincoat